A STORY OF
GOD
AND ALL OF US

YOUNG READERS EDITION

A STORY OF
GOD
AND ALL OF US

YOUNG READERS EDITION

A NOVEL BASED ON
THE EPIC TV MINISERIES

THE
BIBLE

ROMA DOWNEY
~ AND ~
# MARK BURNETT

LITTLE, BROWN AND COMPANY

NEW YORK   BOSTON

Little, Brown and Company

Hachette Book Group
237 Park Avenue, New York, NY 10017
Visit our website at www.lb-kids.com

Little, Brown and Company is a division of Hachette Book Group, Inc.
The Little, Brown name and logo are trademarks of Hachette Book Group, Inc.

The publisher is not responsible for websites (or their content)
that are not owned by the publisher.

First Edition: February 2013
First International Edition: February 2013

Library of Congress Control Number: 2012954964

ISBN 978-0-316-22789-6 (hc) / ISBN 978-0-316-24383-4 (international)

10 9 8 7 6 5 4 3 2 1

RRD-C

Printed in the United States of America

"Let your light shine before others,
that they may see your good deeds
and glorify your Father in heaven."

MATTHEW 5:16

TABLE OF CONTENTS

A NOTE TO PARENTS

In the spring of 2011 we began work on a ten-hour television miniseries: *The Bible*. It would begin with the Book of Genesis and end with the Book of Revelation. As you can imagine, we were immediately faced with a massive creative challenge: how do we tell this story? More specifically: how do we transform a sacred narrative that spans thousands of years and features hundreds of individual stories into just ten hours of television?

We had one of two choices: either select dozens of short summaries and tell many brief stories, or choose fewer characters and stories but make a much deeper emotional connection.

Clearly, we had to go with the second choice.

So we began the TV scripts, written by a team of writers under the guidance of many theologians, advisors, and biblical experts. Their combined expertise brought forth vivid spiritual and historical images. To our great joy, when we showed the scripts to others for technical and creative feedback, the resounding messages we heard over and over were "I've never been able to imagine these Bible stories so clearly in my mind," "I'm going to reread the Bible," and "You really should publish these scripts."

Initially we were resistant, but then we started researching. We came across startling facts like: half of Americans cannot name the first five books of the Bible; 12 percent of American Christians believe that Noah's wife was Joan of Arc; and many believe that Sodom and Gomorrah were a married couple. If our scripts had provided an impetus for people to want to reread the Bible and given them a clearer picture of these stories, then maybe by novelizing the scripts we could spark even more people to pick up the Bible.

Thus, we began the novel *A Story of God and All of Us*, and here we have adapted it for the young reader. We feel very inadequate to teach the Bible, and we are certainly not theologians. We are television storytellers. It will be easy for people to focus on how we have "compressed stories" or to find "theological inaccuracies." But on this point, we must be clear: we are not retelling the story of the Bible; it has already been told in the richest, fullest way possible, from the mouth of

God and through his chosen prophets, apostles, and students. Instead, we are dramatizing some of these beautiful stories from our scripts.

We owe a huge debt of thanks to the small army of scriptwriters, our amazing production team, and all of our advisors and biblical experts. We also want to thank you for holding this novel in your hands. Our television miniseries will be seen by millions around the world, and it is our hope that the series, together with this book, will inspire many more millions to read and reread the greatest story ever told: the Bible.

Roma Downey and Mark Burnett
California, 2013

FOREWORD

Have you ever wondered why the powerful and inspiring stories of the Bible stay in our hearts long after we first learn them? Perhaps it's because they continue to resonate within us. We recognize ourselves in the stories; we see our own lives play out in the situations. We identify with the struggles and the victories, the sorrows and the joys. We see them all as relevant to ourselves.

And they are. These are our stories.

Whatever we may face in our lives today, we can rely on the stories of the Bible to help shine a light on the answers we need. I believe this is one of God's most important gifts to us.

It has been my privilege to help tell the stories of these great biblical figures. Most of us may already be familiar with many of these characters from church, readings, and teachings. But when we experience these old familiar stories told in new ways, they become alive in us and stay vivid and fresh in our minds and our hearts.

The story of Jesus is a story of love, for God so loved the world that he gave his one and only son. The struggles and sacrifices that Noah, Abraham, Moses, David, and Mary endured thousands of years ago are all stories from our shared experience of God's love. We see ourselves in these people. Throughout *A Story of God and All of Us*, you will see that these people lived with the same fears, hopes, loves, and joys that we all have.

They are just like us. It is, after all, a story we share.

My dream is that the courage and love these people inspired in me will reach through history yet again and inspire you.

Love and Light,
Roma

PROLOGUE

Let there be light!" God's voice booms.

A bolt of brightness creates the heavens. And with that light comes wind, sweeping across the brand-new universe. Then water, seemingly endless, soaks everything.

God parts the waters, creating the seas and the sky and the land.

He decrees that plants and seeds and trees cover the land and that there be seasons. And stars in the sky. And creatures throughout the land and waters.

Then God creates man in his own image. Then woman, because man should not be alone. Their names are Adam and Eve, and they inhabit a paradise known as Eden.

All this takes six days in God's time.

On the seventh day, God rests.

God's perfect creation, humankind, becomes flawed

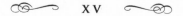

by those who turn their backs on their Creator. First Eve, then Adam, then Cain, and on and on. Generations pass, and devotion to God has all but disappeared. Evil rules in the hearts of men and women. This does not please the Creator, who loves the earth and its people and wants only what's best for them.

So God is starting over. He is destroying mankind in order to save it.

It is night. A large wooden ship bobs on a storm-tossed sea. A howling wind and pelting rain threaten to sink the homemade vessel. Inside the ship, an oil lamp swings from the ceiling and lights a birdcage filled with two brightly colored parrots. An old man named Noah struggles to remain seated. His wife sits next to him. On the other side of the cabin, Noah's three terrified sons hold tight to their wives as the great ship heaves in the night.

From belowdecks, they hear the bellows of oxen, the whinnies of horses, the bleatings of sheep, and countless other animal cries of distress. There are precisely two of each type of beast and bird.

A geyser of water spurts through a new leak in the hull. The women scream. Noah battles to stand and plug the hole. Outside the ship, a blue whale breaches. It is an enormous animal, and yet it is dwarfed by Noah's ark.

Noah is a strong leader, a loving husband, and a good father. He keeps his terrified family calm by telling them the story of creation—a story he knows well.

"On the third day," Noah says calmly, "God created the land, with trees and plants—"

"Will we ever see land again?" asks the wife of Noah's son Shem.

Noah ignores her. "...with trees and plants and fruit. And—"

"Will we?" the woman insists.

Noah's faith is at its very limit. Yet he puts on a brave face. "Of course." He continues his narrative, if only because it gives them comfort. "And on the fifth day... all the creatures of the sea...and of the air. Then on the *sixth* day, all the creatures of the ground—which includes us! And we were granted paradise. Amazing, isn't it? Paradise. But then..." Noah pauses and gathers himself.

"Adam and Eve threw it all away! They ate from the one tree in paradise from which they were forbidden to eat. That was all God asked. Nothing more. Don't—eat—from—this—tree. What could be easier? Wrong choices," he says bitterly. "This is the source of all evil—disobeying God. That's why, with one simple act, Adam and Eve caused evil to enter the world. That's why we are on this ship. Because the evil that Adam and Eve introduced has spread throughout the world, and God is cleaning the earth so mankind can start all over." He looks around the small cabin at the few people who fill it. His story has taken their minds off the storm, and he feels encouraged to keep talking. "That's why God told me, 'Build an ark.'" Noah pauses, remembering the humor in that moment. "I asked, 'What is an ark?' God told me, 'It is the same as a boat.' And I said to God, 'What is a boat?'"

Everyone laughs. They have lived in a desert their whole lives—not much water, let alone a need to build a special craft to float upon it.

God described the ark to Noah. It would be designed and built according to specifications that God dictated. This enormous ship would hold two of each animal. Once it was complete, God would soak the world in a massive storm, flooding all the lands and killing all of God's creation. Only the people and animals aboard Noah's ark would live.

Noah built the ship, even though his friends mocked him and his own wife thought him a fool. Why, he was miles from the nearest water, with no way to launch his vessel. Yet Noah kept building, one nail and one board at a time, constructing pens to house the tigers and elephants and lions and rhinoceroses. His great ship towered above the desert floor and could be seen from miles away. Noah and his ark were a great joke, told far and wide, and many people made the journey to see the ark—if only to shake their heads and chuckle at Noah's folly.

Then the first drop of rain fell. That first drop was not an ordinary trifle of rain, for it hit the earth with a mighty splat that foretold the coming of doom. The skies turned from the clearest blue to gray and then to black. "Go into the ark," God commanded Noah. He obeyed and brought his family on board.

The rains that poured down were unending. The waters grew higher as subterranean rivers burst up through the earth's surface. Great tidal waves surged across the land. Flash floods wiped away homes, markets, and villages.

And as the land slowly disappeared, to be replaced far and wide by only water, Noah closed the hatch, knocked away the supports. Soon the water lifted his massive ship—which floated quite well, much to his relief—and they bobbed away, bound for only God knew where. But one thing was certain: God would save them from destruction, no matter how bad the storms and how high the seas.

Noah's story has had its desired effect. Everyone in the small cabin is now calm. Noah goes up on deck alone, and for the first time in what seems like months, the seas are calm.

Noah now revels in the warmth of the sun on his face. The ark is bobbing toward land. Then he hears God's voice loud and clear, and he knows his journey is over.

"Come out of the ark," God commands.

The great door on the side of the ark is lowered. The animals pour out onto the dry land and quickly scatter.

God has saved the world by nearly destroying it. Noah was chosen to continue God's plans for humanity. But humankind is destined to make the same mistakes.

God will act once again to save the world. But next time he will not need a Noah.

Next time he will send his only son.

This is a story of God and all of us.

PART ONE

A Man Named
Abraham

Thousands of years ago, in the city of Ur, in modern-day Iraq, lives a man named Abram, a direct descendant of Noah. Abram is a healthy seventy-five years old, with broad shoulders and a flowing, dark beard. His wife Sarai is known far and wide for her great beauty. The one sadness of their otherwise charmed lives is that Sarai has not been able to have children. One could never detect this sorrow from Abram's behavior. He is always quick with a smile, and forever has a "Peace be with you" on his lips.

One day, in the temple, he hears a voice he has never heard before. It is speaking only to Abram; no one else can hear it.

"Abram." It is the voice of God. "Leave your country, your people, and your father's household, and go to the land I will show you."

Abram gazes up to the sky, his mouth open in shock.

"I will make you into a great nation, and I will bless you. I will make your name great, and you will be a blessing. I will bless those who bless you, and whoever curses you I will curse. And all the peoples on earth will be blessed through you."

A lesser man would be puzzled. Or perhaps fearful. But Abram hears the call, which is why God picked him for the task he has in mind.

"Yes," Abram softly tells God, in a voice brimming with passion. "Yes."

Abram races home from the temple. He finds his wife at the back of the house and takes her into his arms. "Sarai, today God has spoken to me."

"Which God?"

"*The* God."

Sarai pulls back, confused. Theirs is a world of many different gods and idols, each designed to fulfill a specific need.

"I speak the truth," Abram promises. "He has chosen me. Chosen *us*."

"For what? I do not understand."

"He wants us to leave here."

"Leave? But our whole life is here."

"Yes, Sarai. Leave. We are going away from this city to a new land. And we will have children in that new land. Of that I am sure. God has promised."

Although he is asking her to do something extra-ordinary, something unimaginable, she knows she must trust him.

Sarai squeezes Abram's hand and smiles. "Take us there."

Abram sets out with Sarai, his nephew Lot and his wife, and a small group of friends and servants. They travel north and west, following the ancient roads of what we now call the Fertile Crescent, trusting God to lead them to the land he has promised Abram. Their journey takes them through a city known as Haran and finally to a bountiful land of water and palm trees that offers a green oasis in an otherwise barren desert. But the land is not enough for all of Abram's party and their animals. Making matters worse, seeds of dissension are sown by Lot's wife, a jealous and small-hearted woman who chafes at Abram's authority for forcing her to relocate. It soon becomes a standoff, with Abram and his followers on one side, and the followers of his beloved nephew Lot on the other. Finally, after much conflict, Lot tells his uncle, whom he loves like a father, that he and his tribe must leave the larger group for greener pastures, for the wretched and sinful city of Sodom. It is a sad time.

Years pass.

Abram is now ninety-nine years old. Sarai is ninety. They now live in an oasis near a place called Mamre—amid palm, cedar, and fig trees and clear running water—still dwelling in the tents they have called home for so many years. This is not paradise, nor is it the land Abram envisioned when he and his followers, who some call Hebrews, struck out on their own so long ago. One hot afternoon, as Abram sits before his tent, the Lord appears to him. "I am God Almighty," he tells Abram, who falls facedown on the ground.

"I will confirm my covenant between me and you," God continues. "And I will greatly increase your numbers."

God orders that Abram change his name to Abraham, which means "father of many nations." From now on, Sarai will be called Sarah, for "princess." And then God makes an outrageous promise to Abraham: Sarah will give birth to a son. "She will be the mother of nations. Kings of peoples will come down from her."

Abraham laughs at the idea. He does not believe that Sarah can give birth. But God insists, and says that a long line of earthly kings will be brought forth from this lineage.

The words settle on Abraham's heart, filling him with a joy he has never known. He cannot wait to tell

Sarah. Abraham turns to God to offer his thanks. But God has already gone.

One day not long after, Abraham sees three powerful and mysterious men in the distance walking toward his camp. They wear robes made of fine fabric. On two of the men he can see the outlines of weapons beneath their garments, yet they do not appear menacing. Instead, they have the quietly intense presence of holy men. Abraham feels an instant connection with them, and as is his custom, he enjoys playing the part of the good host. Yet these men are somehow different, and he treats them with more respect.

Abraham's instincts are correct. Two of the men are angels. The third is God disguised in flesh. Abraham has heard God's voice but does not recognize him.

"Welcome," says Abraham. "You are most welcome. Please sit down." He indicates a spot where they can rest in the shade.

"Are you hungry?" he asks. Without waiting for an answer, Abraham orders a servant to bring food.

"Have you traveled far?" Abraham continues.

"Yes, a very long way," answers one of the angels. A long silence ensues.

"Where is your wife?" asks the other angel.

Abraham points to their tent. "In there."

Inside the fabric walls of their tent, Sarah hears

strange voices, but she is weary and in no mood to entertain travelers.

The Lord then speaks: "I will surely return to you about this time next year, and Sarah, your wife, will have a son."

Sarah laughs to herself as she overhears this. Surely this man, whoever he is, does not know that Abraham's wife is very advanced in age and cannot have children.

"Why did you laugh?" the Lord says to her.

Sarah almost jumps out of her skin. She whirls around to see who is speaking to her, but no one is in the tent. *I didn't laugh*, she thinks to herself.

"You did," the Lord says. His voice is kind. Once again, Sarah spins quickly to see who is playing this trick. But she is alone.

God continues: "So you will never forget how you doubted me, when you have a son, you will name him Isaac, which means 'laughter.'"

Sarah feels the power of God and is overcome with hope. Tears stream down her face. She falls to her knees and thanks God.

The time comes for the three strangers to leave. Abraham has treated them with extreme kindness and deference. He has brought them water to wash the road dust off their feet. He has cooked them a fatted calf and fed them a meal featuring curds, milk, and thin loaves of bread. These powerful, mysterious strangers are special, and Abraham has reveled in the honor of their presence. He referred to himself as their servant and even stood off to one side as they dined, waiting to be summoned. The men have maintained their air of mystery, saying little else as they enjoyed the food and the shade. As the afternoon sun grows cool they stand to depart.

"Where are you going?" Abraham asks cautiously, still unaware of whom he has been entertaining.

One of the angels looks to God for permission to answer.

God nods.

"We are going to decide the fate of Sodom," the angel replies solemnly, pulling his hood up over his head. The other angel does the same, and they depart, leaving God alone with Abraham, who is very concerned because Lot lives in Sodom.

God walks with Abraham to a mountaintop, where they can look out and see Sodom in the distance.

"Shall I hide from you what I am going to do?" the Lord wonders aloud. "You will surely become a great and powerful nation, and all nations on earth will be blessed through you. For I have chosen you so that you will direct your children and your household after you to keep the way of the Lord by doing what is right and just, so that I will bring about for you what I have promised."

Abraham is stunned to realize that he stands in the presence of God. It can be no one else. This is the manner in which God has spoken to him so many times. And Abraham is just as stunned to realize that the destruction of Sodom will mean the death of Lot. Despite their differences, Abraham loves Lot like a son and is in dread for his safety.

Abraham musters up his courage and speaks to the Lord. "Will you sweep away the righteous with the wicked?"

"If I find ten righteous people in the city of Sodom, I will spare the whole city for their sake," replies God.

But there are not ten righteous people in all of Sodom. In fact, there is just one—Lot. Only he and his children will be saved.

Soon, on a hillside overlooking the city, a horrified Abraham witnesses the flames shooting upward through the buildings as the city begins to burn. Fireballs continue to rain down from above, joined by lightning and the unnerving boom of thunder.

Behind him, unseen, stands God.

———

Time passes: Abraham paces nervously until he hears the sound of a newborn infant breathing its first gulps of air. He pulls back the tent flap. A beaming Sarah holds their child to her chest. Abraham leans down to her. Without saying a word, she hands him the child. Tears well in the corners of his eyes as he holds the baby.

"A boy," Sarah whispers. She is radiant.

"Just as God promised," Abraham marvels. "Just as God promised. Only the Almighty can do the impossible."

Abraham holds the child aloft. "His name will be Isaac." He and Sarah burst into joyous laughter.

———

Ten more years pass.

Isaac emerges from his family's tent, with its tasseled doorway and striped fabric walls. He yawns and stretches as he makes his way past the goat pen and over to the cooking fire, where Sarah grinds grain to make flour for the morning bread.

Abraham has been awake for hours. His age is truly beginning to show, and though he slept the night through, he is extremely tired. Weary. Abraham sees his life slipping away. He doesn't feel like the leader God intended him to be. He doesn't feel worthy of God, of the Promised Land, or of the prospect that his descendants will be as numerous as the stars. As he gets older with each passing day, Abraham ponders his purpose.

The wind picks up and blows the grain into the fire. The wind grows louder. Abraham looks all around and notices that he is alone. Everyone in the camp, including Sarah and Isaac, has disappeared.

It has been a long time since God spoke to Abraham, but he still knows the voice well. "A sacrifice?" he whispers to God.

It is common for Abraham to offer sacrifices to God. In his ritual, an animal is offered as a sign of thanks.

God goes on to tell him the details.

At first Abraham doesn't comprehend what he's hearing. Then, as he realizes what God is saying, he becomes horrified. "No," he whispers. "Please, no. Haven't I shown enough faith? Dear God, I will make any sacrifice you ask. Anything"—now he can barely speak—"anything but Isaac."

⟨◦⟩

It is God's will. With a heavy heart, Abraham retrieves his best knife from his tent. He and his people are camped at the foot of a great desert peak, Mount Moriah. As the sun rises higher and higher in the sky, Abraham sets off in search of Isaac, his knife firmly secured in the sheath on his waist.

He finds him eating bread with Sarah. "Eat more," she encourages the boy. "How will you ever grow if you don't eat?" But she stops talking as Abraham draws near.

"God wants a sacrifice," Abraham says, offering a hand to Isaac. "Come with me," he commands.

"Of course," Isaac says brightly, and then rushes off to gather his bag for the long and arduous trip up Mount Moriah.

Storm clouds are rolling in, and Abraham and Isaac can hear the faint boom of approaching thunder. The two gather wood for a fire along the way, and with each twig and branch that Isaac presents to his father, Abraham finds himself more and more distraught about what he must do. God has demanded this beautiful, innocent boy as a sacrifice.

"Father?" Isaac asks, handing him a new handful of twigs.

Abraham takes them. "Good work," he tells his son. "Let's get more."

Soon the bundle is so thick that Abraham wraps it in rope and straps it to Isaac's back so the wood can be carried more easily. Abraham then makes another bundle, which he shoulders for the hike to the summit. "Enough sticks," he tells Isaac. "Let's just get up there."

"But why are we going directly to the top?" Isaac asks. "We have the firewood for the sacrifice, but we still need to go back down and get the lamb."

Abraham sighs. His heart is heavy. "God will provide the sacrifice, my son."

Up on the mountain, the storm grows fiercer. The sun, strangely, is completely white, and then the sky turns black. Winds swirl. Clouds seem low and thick enough to touch. Abraham knows there can be no greater sacrifice than for a father to offer his son. This is the most difficult test of faith he has ever endured.

When the time comes to do what he must do, a

voice calls out to him. Abraham sees an angel standing near a bush.

"Abraham! Do not hurt your son," the angel tells him. "You have proved that you have faith in God. The Lord will bless you with descendants as numerous as the stars in the heavens."

Abraham turns from the angel to look at Isaac. Isaac looks off to where the angel stood. But the angel is not there anymore.

Years after his death, Abraham's great-grandsons will found the twelve tribes of Israel. The nation will be called Israel because their father, Jacob, is also known as Israel. This does not ensure harmony throughout the land, or even a powerful kingdom, for there is great bitterness and rivalry among the brothers. Jacob makes no secret of the fact that the eleventh son, Joseph, is his favorite.

Just as Abraham once discovered, every group, large or small, needs wise leadership—and this is where Jacob is found wanting. Jacob lacks the sense to treat all his sons equally. A symbol of Jacob's love for Joseph is a splendid multicolored robe. Given to Joseph as a gift, the robe has come to signify all that the brothers loathe about him. It would be wise for Joseph not to wear the robe at all, but he cannot help himself. This only makes his brothers more furious.

One day, in the fields outside the family estate, the brothers gather around Joseph. They trip him and then circle around him as he lies in the dust. Simeon, one of the older brothers, angrily pulls at the elaborate coat.

"We'll have that," he demands.

"No," Joseph answers defiantly.

This is followed by the sound of fabric being ripped. All the brothers laugh and pull eagerly at the coat as Joseph cries out in anguish. They push his face down into the dirt. Their sandaled feet kick dust upon him.

"Look!" cries Judah, one of the brothers.

Joseph peers into the distance and instantly knows his fate. It becomes obvious that Joseph's brothers mean to do him even greater harm. For he sees a line of pack animals and a single-file line of men roped together. This is a slave caravan, headed through Israel on its way to Egypt with a fresh cargo of men to sell.

Joseph's tattered robe lies on the cracked earth. Simeon and the other brothers drop the blood of a dead goat upon the robe until it is drenched. Then, adopting their most solemn and forlorn faces, the brothers approach their father with some very bad news.

Simeon pulls back the flap to Jacob's tent and presents the robe to his father. "No...," Jacob says, a smile vanishing from his face. He puts his hand through one of the holes in the fabric. "A wild beast did this?"

Simeon shrugs helplessly. "It must have been. We didn't see what happened."

"Why?" Jacob yells to the heavens. "Why, O Lord?"

He buries his face in the robe. Benjamin—at ten years old, the youngest of his sons—looks on helplessly. He has been sworn to silence and knows better than to cross his brothers. Jacob's face is covered in tears. His favorite son is gone.

Joseph is sold to a wealthy Egyptian family, but his life seems to go from bad to worse after a misunderstanding, and he is cast out of the house and thrown into prison. Time passes, and he becomes thin and sickly from months in the filthy conditions.

Yet Joseph is an optimistic and warmhearted man, even in the toughest of times. He soon becomes friends with his cellmates, both of whom once worked in the royal palace—one as a cupbearer, the other as a baker. Joseph has a gift for listening to God, prayerfully and intently. This enables him to interpret the meanings of dreams. During his time in prison, Joseph is not afraid to share this gift.

"And what does my dream mean?" the baker asks him one morning. The three men sit on the grubby cell floor, chains clanking whenever they try to move. "The one with the birds and the baskets?"

Joseph closes his eyes to concentrate. "You were carrying three baskets of bread?"

"Yes! Then the birds attacked me and ate the bread!"

Joseph focuses. "In three days' time..." He lifts his head and looks hard at the baker. "You will be executed," Joseph informs him solemnly. And to the cupbearer, "You will be freed."

The execution comes to pass, just as Joseph predicts. The cupbearer is soon released from prison, leaving Joseph alone in his cell. He spends his days on his knees in prayer, trying to divine God's plan for his life. Man's relationship with God seems impossible to fathom, but Joseph feels as if God is watching over him.

Light floods into Joseph's cell one day as a jailer steps in to wash the filth from his body. Joseph's heart sinks, for he knows that being bathed can mean only one thing: an appointment to see the Pharaoh—which, of course, also means execution.

Soon Joseph's hands are bound behind his back. He is led out of the jail and into the Pharaoh's throne room. A foreigner, a prisoner, and a slave, Joseph knows that his life has no value to the Pharaoh. And yet he stands tall, placing his faith in God.

Pharaoh enters the room and sits on his throne. He nods and Joseph hears the clank of a sword being pulled. But instead of feeling its sharp tip press against his back, Joseph is stunned to feel the ropes being cut from his wrists. The flat of the sword then smacks against Joseph's legs, driving him down onto his knees.

The cupbearer whom Joseph knew in prison steps forth and offers the Pharaoh a drink. Pharaoh accepts, sipping slowly before clearing his throat to speak. "I've had strange dreams," he tells Joseph. "My magicians can't explain them. But I'm told that you can."

"No," Joseph says, his face pressed to the ground. "God can. Through me."

"Whose god?" Pharaoh asks, his voice dripping in scorn. "Your God?"

Joseph dares to look up. "What is your dream?" he asks boldly. The flat of the sword smacks him on the back of the neck, forcing him to gaze down once again.

This is where he stays as he listens to the Pharaoh describe his dream.

"I was by the Nile," begins the Pharaoh, "when out of the river came seven cows, fat and healthy. Then seven thin, ugly cows swallowed them whole. Then I had a different dream. Seven full heads of wheat, glowing in the sun—then quickly eaten by seven rotten ones, thin and scorched by the wind." He drinks thoughtfully. "Can your God explain that?"

Joseph is silent, lost in prayer. He waits patiently for the voice of God. Just as Pharaoh is about to lose all patience, Joseph speaks, his gaze still directed at the stone floor. "The cows and grain are all the same," he says.

"What do you mean?"

"There will be seven years of plenty. But then seven years of famine. You must store food in preparation for that day."

"There will be no famine," the Pharaoh says imperiously. "The Nile always feeds our crops. Every year, without fail."

"You don't understand: there *will* be famine," Joseph explains.

"You contradict the Pharaoh?"

Joseph speaks carefully, knowing that his next words could be his last. "You contradict your dream."

"Go on."

"Store grain. Store a portion of the harvest when it is plentiful. Otherwise your people will starve. This is the meaning of your dream."

Pharaoh rises and steps down from his throne. "I am impressed by your conviction. You are set free, but on one condition."

"What is that, Pharaoh?"

"You will be in charge of telling the people to store their harvest."

Joseph's prophecy is proved correct. Thanks to the power given him by the Pharaoh, Joseph is able to force farmers throughout Egypt to store their crops.

For Joseph, this dramatic change of fortune is divine providence. He will forever remember it as a message that there is always hope, even in the darkest moments. Thanks to his success, he assimilates into Egyptian society and becomes one of its most powerful men. A signet ring is placed upon his finger. Eyeliner decorates his eyes, preventing the sun's strong rays from burning them. He wears a black, straight-haired wig, and his chin is always smoothly shaved.

Thanks to Joseph, Pharaoh's wealth increases

massively—though at the expense of many Egyptians, who are forced to sell their land to survive the famine. And it is not just Egypt that suffers through the seven-year drought. The people of neighboring nations feel the pain as their crops wither and die. Thousands upon thousands of foreigners flood into Egypt, which has become legendary for its well-stocked granaries. Among them are Joseph's brothers, sent there by Jacob to purchase grain. To do anything less would mean the end of their lineage, for they would all starve in Israel.

So it is that Joseph sees his brothers in a crowd as he makes his way by chariot through a busy city street one day. He immediately orders that they be sent to his palace. Joseph has never talked about the painful method in which his brothers changed his life, but he has also never forgotten. Now he has the ability to change their lives—for better or worse—as they once changed his.

Joseph's brothers are led into a formal drawing room by armed guards. Joseph enters the room with all the regal grace he has learned during his long rise to power. In his black wig and eyeliner, he is unrecognizable to his brothers. They cower as Joseph studies their faces. He can do anything he wants to them right now. Yet Joseph's thoughts are always upon God. He shows his brothers the same love and mercy God has always shown him, particularly when times were so hard that hope barely flickered in his soul.

"Feed them," Joseph orders.

His brothers are shocked. This act of kindness goes beyond their wildest dreams. As soon as they are able, the brothers make their way out of the room. Outside, their donkeys are being loaded with heaping bags of grain to take home to Israel. Not once do they suspect that Joseph is their brother.

But Joseph is not done with them. His kindness comes with a price, for he wants to know whether his brothers have changed their ways and learned compassion for others. Joseph has contrived a test: hidden within one of those bags of grain is a silver goblet. Guards have been instructed to slice open the bag and reveal this cup and charge his brothers with theft. This is where the test begins.

Everything goes according to plan. Simeon, Judah, Benjamin, and the others wait patiently as their donkeys are loaded with sacks of grain. When the brothers are ready to leave, a guard pretends to notice something suspicious and slices open a bag to examine the strange bulge. The silver cup falls onto the ground. Joseph's brothers are grabbed and immediately marched back to stand before him.

They kneel once again, this time even more terrified than before.

"I am told that this man is the guilty party," Joseph tells them, staring at Benjamin. He has carefully selected the youngest to blame, for he alone among the brothers was blameless when Joseph was sold into slavery.

"Benjamin would never steal," Simeon begs.

"Silence!" barks Joseph. "Go home. All of you. But this one stays—as my slave."

The brothers all raise their faces, begging together. "No!" they cry out. "Please! We beg of you!"

Joseph surveys them with amusement.

"We cannot leave him," protests Judah.

"It would destroy our father!" agrees Simeon.

"I will be your slave instead," adds Judah. To which Simeon protests that he should be the one taken into slavery.

"Silence!" Joseph commands once again. He struggles to remain composed. All the brothers fearfully press their faces to the floor. With a wave, Joseph dismisses all his guards. They leave. He stands alone, towering over his brothers.

"Bring our father here," he says in a hoarse whisper.

A mystified Simeon sneaks a look at Joseph, who has removed his wig.

"Joseph?" asks Simeon, stunned. The others raise their eyes.

Joseph has longed so many years for this moment. "What you did to me was wrong," he tells his brothers. "But God made it right. He watched over me. I have saved many lives, thanks to him."

⌒⌒⌒

The brothers do as they are told, returning home and bringing Jacob to Egypt so that he might be reunited with his son. The entire family is together again—all of Israel's children. But they are in the wrong place, and they know it. For while they now live in luxury, this is not the land that God promised Abraham.

Even worse, over the generations that follow, the drought Joseph predicted means that thousands upon thousands are forced to leave. The people of Israel travel to Egypt in search of food, and eventually become enslaved. They build the great palaces and monuments of Egypt, working all day under the blazing desert sun. They are slaves of a great Pharaoh.

But they will be saved by an outcast, a man who will have an extraordinary relationship with God.

This man's name is Moses.

PART TWO

EXODUS

Almost five hundred years have passed since Abraham died. His descendants are hundreds of miles from the Promised Land, and a generation from ever setting eyes upon it. They are slaves in the land of Egypt, but they are also a proud and strong people. As God promised, they have become as numerous as the stars in the skies—so numerous, in fact, that the Egyptian Pharaoh is afraid there will be a rebellion. So he has sent his soldiers throughout the land—village to village, house to house—to kill every Hebrew baby boy.

Yet one brave Jewish woman is taking extraordinary measures to save her child. For three long months she has successfully hidden her boy from the Egyptian soldiers. Now she fights for her baby's life by wrapping him in a blanket and concealing him in a basket. The simple basket is this nameless mother's version of

Noah's ark. Just as God sent Noah to save the world, she has fashioned a second ark that will carry a boy who will become a man and continue the job that Noah began.

Then comes the hard part—so hard that she cannot bear to witness it herself. Instead, she sends her daughter, Miriam, to hide the basket in the reeds along the Nile's edge, knowing that a number of terrible things might happen to her child.

Miriam doesn't want to do this, but she has no choice. Either she hides her brother in the reeds, or he is sure to die at the hands of Egyptian soldiers. Better to do something—even something foolish—than to let her brother be pulled from her mother's breast and hurled into the dark blue waters of the Nile. Now she watches helplessly. She tries to remain calm as she follows the little ark along the water's edge.

Miriam bites her lip in anticipation as the basket holding the boy bobs nearer and nearer to where the Pharaoh's daughter Batya bathes.

Miriam's heart soars as Batya lifts the young boy from the basket and clumsily attempts to cradle him. Batya is too young to have a child of her own, knows nothing about holding or taking care of a baby, and immediately knows that this child is an Israelite slave.

"Please put it back, my lady," requests a maid.

Miriam, a girl of great faith, begins to pray. The princess could easily toss the baby back into the river.

"Please, God, help him," begs Miriam.

God hears Miriam's prayer.

Batya smiles at the baby boy. "This one lives," she proclaims.

"But what will the Pharaoh say?"

"Let me deal with the Pharaoh. This is my boy now. And I shall name him Moses." Moses, the Egyptian name meaning "drawn out of the water."

Miriam rushes to her mother and tells of Moses' new home. Her mother cries out in joy. Her son will live.

Prince Moses stares straight forward as his maid-servant applies black kohl eyeliner. Moses is a muscular young man, full of ideals and optimism. He has grown up in the Pharaoh's court as a grandson and never known a day of fear, worry, or hardship. His every wish is granted and every whim catered to—most unlike the Hebrew slaves who toil for Pharaoh, from whom he is unknowingly descended. Few know Moses' true story, least of all Moses himself.

The servant moves behind Moses to fasten the amulet

around his neck, as he does every morning. This talisman is meant to guarantee safety and good luck, though given Moses' luxurious surroundings, wearing it is more of a ritual to appease the many gods of Egypt.

Batya, his mother, enters his dressing room looking very worried. "Moses," she says wearily, "I hope you're not going to fight again."

The prince stands, dressed for combat.

"He keeps challenging me, Mother," Moses says calmly.

"So refuse him!"

The clang of swords soon echoes through the palace courtyard. On one side of the arena is Moses, a skilled and careful swordsman with a deep competitive streak. On the other is a son of Rameses and heir to the Egyptian throne. Both are armed with a sword and shield. They are both nothing more than teenage boys.

"I've been practicing," young Rameses cries with false bravado. His teeth are gritted as he warily circles Moses, eyes fixed on his opponent's sword.

"We don't have to do this," Moses says evenly.

"Yes, we do," Rameses vows, feeling the thick beads of sweat coursing down his forehead and into his eyes.

"You may be my sister's favorite, but I am the next in line to my father's throne—and don't forget it," Rameses continues.

When Rameses sees that Moses has no intention of fighting back, he attempts attack after attack, hacking down hard on Moses' shield with his sword. Moses even falls to one knee as a sign that this duel is senseless, but the attacks continue.

"Ha!" cries Rameses. "I made you kneel!"

Moses stands. He holds up his shield but lets his sword dangle uselessly to the ground. "Enough. I don't want to hurt you."

"Fight me, Moses. I command you!"

But Moses turns his back. An enraged Rameses runs at him and attacks Moses from behind. This violates every rule of combat. Fed up with Rameses' behavior, Moses turns and fights. Moses strikes blow after blow on Rameses' shield and says, like an older brother, "I will not tolerate this foolish behavior any longer."

Rameses falls to one knee and cowers behind his shield, hoping Moses doesn't take the next step and kill him.

Pharaoh arrives just in time to see Moses embarrassing his son, making the future Pharaoh look weak and unfit. Batya and several palace courtiers are at his side, witnesses to Rameses' shame. Word will soon spread in the palace and throughout the nearby villages, and make it apparent that Moses should be the next Pharaoh.

"Stop!" thunders Pharaoh's voice.

Moses turns from Rameses and looks to Pharaoh.

Rameses screams at Moses in pain. "You will pay for this! I will be Pharaoh. I will be god!" He then turns to his father. "It is your fault. You should have never let her keep him," Rameses screams. Then, a final jab at Moses: "You're not even one of us!"

"He's right," Pharaoh tells Batya.

Moses stares at his mother, who looks away. The truth is starting to dawn on him. "What's he talking about?"

"Tell him," Pharaoh orders his daughter. With that, Pharaoh and a smirking Rameses leave the arena, followed by a small army of unnerved courtiers.

A most confused Prince Moses is left alone with Batya. "Tell me what, Mother?" he asks, not sure if he wants to know the answer.

A tear falls down Batya's cheek. "Moses, I love you like a son. But you are not my blood."

"Then who...is my mother?" he mumbles in shock. "Where did I come from?"

Batya takes him to a window. In the distance they can see the Hebrews laboring in the hot sun. "The slaves, Moses. You were a slave child. I saved you. You also have a brother. And a sister. But they are not like you and me. They worship the God of their ancestor Abraham, and he has deserted them."

"And my real mother? Where is she?"

Batya falls silent. Moses rushes out of the room. He must see these people—*his* people—for himself.

Moses watches men, women, and children labor in the blazing sun. The heat is like an inferno. Their faces are weary and their spirits are broken. His people are without a hope or a future. In his eighteen years in the Pharaoh's court, Moses has never paid these people any heed. They have always been beneath him, a separate people he never noticed. Until now, he has never known or witnessed the cruelty they suffer in daily existence. His heart is in conflict, for this could easily have been him. Somewhere among them is a family he has never known.

Moses hears an anguished shout: "No!" He turns to see an Israelite slave being dragged into the shadows of a nearby building. "Please, no," the slave screams. Moses follows the sound into a blind corner, where he finds a slave master beating a young man with a large club.

"Filthy slave," sneers the overseer, spitting on the Hebrew.

He lands blow after blow, even though the man cowers and tries to cover his face. Moses doesn't know what to do. This is not his business. The slave surely did something to deserve these painful blows. As the stick rises into the air and comes down again and again, Moses can no longer be an innocent bystander. Without fully realizing what he is doing, Prince Moses—a resident of the great Pharaoh's palace and recognized throughout the land as the son of Batya—walks back toward the slave master and picks up a large stone. He approaches the slave master from behind and raises the rock high over his head.

The slave master turns just in time to see Moses preparing to attack.

Moses, stunned, stops. He is not sure what to do next. He runs.

⌒⌒⌒

Four decades pass.

Rameses now sits on the Egyptian throne and Moses is a shepherd, living on Mount Sinai. It is a hard, lonely life. His beard is long, and his face is dry and bronzed by the sun. His body is strong from having survived the elements. His mind dwells constantly on his people enslaved in Egypt.

On this day, Moses sees something amazing. A small bush is ablaze. Yet the leaves and branches do not burn. And there is no smell of smoke. It is just a flame, brilliant as the daytime sun.

Moses approaches cautiously. As he does, the flames begin to roar with sound. Moses walks closer. He shields his face with his hand, lest the heat burn him and the light blind him.

In the distance, thunder rolls in a low growl. But in that growl, Moses hears a voice. "Moses! Moses!"

"Here I am," he replies cautiously.

A deafening clap of thunder. Moses raises his hands to his ears, exposing his eyes and face to the intensity of the fiery bush.

"You are real?"

The fire burns so bright that Moses must shield his eyes.

"*I AM*," a voice tells him. "I am the God of your father. The God of Abraham. The God of Isaac. The God of Jacob."

Moses hides his face because he is afraid to look at God. "What do you want with me?" he asks.

Another clap of thunder. This one makes Moses jump back in panic.

"I understand the misery of your people—*my* people. I hear them every night in my dreams. They cry out for freedom," says God.

A loud wind rages. The flames on the bush roar to a new and larger height. But this time, rather than panic, Moses approaches the bush. He hears his instructions, but he is mystified. "Free? How can I set them free? I am not a prince now. I am nothing. Why would they listen to me? I think this is a mistake. There must be someone else."

The fire grows higher in response. Now the flames reach out to Moses, enveloping him. Yet he is not burned. Rather, he feels a new strength course through his veins. He is overcome with a new sense of purpose.

"I'll do it," he says, his voice now resolute. "Who shall I say sent me?"

Moses hears the answer on the wind. In that instant, the fire goes out. The bush, still unburned, lies on the ground.

"Lord," he marvels, rolling the word around on his tongue. "Lord…I will do it, Lord. I will set your people—*my* people—free."

Moses sleeps soundly the rest of the night. In the morning, as the sun rises high in a sky as clear and blue as any he has ever seen, Moses leads his flock into Egypt. He will sell that flock the first chance he gets. For God is about to give him an entirely new kind of flock.

Moses, now an old man, has been given an impossible task: persuade Pharaoh to let those slaves go. They must be set free. "So much suffering," Moses mumbles under his breath, gazing upon men and women who have never known freedom. Caked in dust, emaciated, beaten. These are his people. They are wretched and broken and have no idea what freedom actually means. How is Moses, an outsider who has never lived among them, going to persuade Pharaoh to let them go? And if he does, how is Moses supposed to lead them? The task isn't just impossible. It's unthinkable. Moses is afraid, but he was called upon by God. Only the memory of that burning bush helps him fight his urge to turn around.

"Hey, old man," barks an overseer, before jarring Moses back to reality by shoving him. The slave master raises his whip to beat him, but a powerfully built slave named Joshua intervenes on Moses' behalf just in time.

"Don't worry, sir. Don't worry," Joshua assures the overseer. "I think he's a little confused. Let me take care of this. I am so sorry."

The overseer looks at Moses and Joshua as if they were the dirt itself. He spits into the dust and saunters away, cracking his whip as he goes.

Joshua pulls Moses around a corner. When they're out of sight, Joshua confronts this stranger who has suddenly appeared. "Do you want to get us all a beating?" Joshua hisses at Moses.

Moses only stares at him.

"Who are you?" Joshua asks.

"My name is Moses."

A stunned Joshua takes two steps backward. His eyes glaze over in wonder. "Moses? You are Moses?"

"Yes."

"*The* Moses?"

A deep breath. A reminder that he has not been forgotten. A call to battle. "Yes. *The* Moses."

After meeting with the Israelite slaves, including his siblings, Miriam and Aaron, Moses sends word to the palace that he would like to meet with Rameses. As Moses predicted, the mere mention of his name is enough to produce an audience with the Pharaoh, and soon he and Aaron are escorted up the grand stairway toward Rameses' throne, past ornately carved pillars and statues.

A courtier marches the two Israelites into a large hall. Rameses sits before them on a large golden throne. His son sits by his side in a smaller version of the same regal chair. Moses smiles at the boy, who smiles back.

"You have a son," Moses says to Rameses.

"An heir. My family's dynasty will last forever."

Moses smiles again at the young boy, who shyly looks away. The Pharaoh has a hard look in his eyes. The two men stare at each other, remembering the past.

"Have you come to beg forgiveness?" says an expectant Pharaoh. He has waited years to hear an apology.

The palace guards step forward. If Moses shows disrespect, a simple snap of Pharaoh's finger will see Moses and Aaron thrown to the ground.

"God saved me," Moses explains. "For a purpose."

All around the court, the mood has darkened, for it is clear that Moses is not talking about an Egyptian god but the God of Abraham, whom the Egyptians do not know or worship.

"And what purpose would that be?" the Pharaoh says, amused.

"To demand that you release his people from slavery."

"Demand?" Rameses asks. He steps down from his throne and approaches Moses. The two men stand eye to eye, a Pharaoh and a Hebrew. In any other situation, Moses would have been instantly struck down and killed for daring to look in Pharaoh's eyes. But there is a deep history between these two men, and this is no ordinary moment.

Moses does not back down. "Let my people go."

"You always were a fighter, but you never knew when you were beaten."

Moses weighs his words before responding. "That's because you never beat me. If you defy God, you will receive a punishment more severe than anything I could have ever imagined inflicting upon you."

"I have a good mind to slam my fist hard into your face, Moses," Rameses hisses, "but I will not revisit our childish matches where you always played unfairly. You return, after all these years, to threaten me? Tell me, dear Moses, is it your invisible God who's going to punish *me*? The one who abandons his people? The one who runs from his responsibility, his past...his family?" Rameses beckons to the guards. "Show them who god is!"

The guards shove Moses and Aaron to the hard stone floor.

"I am god!" Rameses shouts in their wake. "I. Am. God."

"No, Rameses," Moses cries out. "You are not God! You are just a man. And you *will* set my people free, so that they may worship with me in the desert!"

⌐‿○

A week later, Moses walks along the banks of the Nile with Miriam and Aaron by his side. He knows that his first real test is upon him. He has made the Pharaoh angry, but God has protected him. He must now convince the Hebrews that God is with them. The Hebrews are a people of faith, but they feel that God has deserted them. Unless God sends a sign, Moses knows, these people will not allow him to speak on their behalf, for fear of the punishment that is sure to follow.

"God has spoken to me," Moses says. "He will make Pharaoh free us—by force, if necessary." Moses turns to Aaron. "We are his agents now, you and I. Are you ready?"

Aaron nods. "That is why he has brought our family together again."

Miriam moves closer to her brothers. "What should we do?"

"We must trust in God. You will see. He will show us the way to go," Moses responds. He finds his way down through the reeds toward the river's edge. His hands touch the rushes and he hesitates a moment. God is talking to him, and Moses knows what to do next. Moses draws himself up, raises his arms to heaven, and points his staff to the sky. Then he turns to Aaron and slowly lowers his staff until it points at his brother. "Put your staff to the water," Moses commands him.

Aaron drops the tip of his staff in the Nile, barely touching the surface. But from that simple point of contact, the water starts to radiate red. The waters of the Nile, the greatest river on earth, flowing thousands upon thousands of miles, have turned to blood.

Moses gazes at the river, not at all surprised by what has just happened. Joshua comes to the bank and looks across, not sure what he is seeing. Is this real?

"God is with us," Moses assures him.

"So surely, Pharaoh will now let us go. Right? He can see for himself what God can do."

"It won't be that easy. This is just the first plague, Joshua. God is sending ten to change Pharaoh's mind."

The next attack soon follows.

Pharaoh's son is one of the first in the palace to notice. He is playing on the floor of his bedroom with his toy chariot when a frog hops past. Then another, and another, all croaking, until a tide of frogs fills the palace. Terrified, the boy climbs onto his bed to escape.

In the throne room, Moses is once again standing before Rameses, repeating God's command that his people be set free. And though the Pharaoh can clearly hear the screams of his son above the croaking, he refuses to back down. "I will not free my slaves," Rameses says, as he stands up and sweeps out of the throne room, followed by his court.

Moses merely shakes his head, for he knows the many trials the Egyptians are about to face. And he knows that with every refusal by Pharaoh, there will come another, more destructive plague.

Next comes the death of all Egypt's livestock—cows, sheep, and goats, the source of their meat and milk. The Egyptian people begin to starve. And still Rameses refuses.

Then the people of Egypt are attacked once again. Hideous boils break out over their skin, as the Israelites are left untouched. And still Rameses refuses to see the truth. A plague of locusts descends, plucking the fields clean of every crop, every bit of grain, and every last morsel of food in the land. Plague after plague visits Egypt, and with each plague, Pharaoh grows more stubborn.

God then finally does to Egypt what Pharaoh once did to Moses' people: he sends his Angel of Death to kill every firstborn son throughout the land. But to ensure that the Angel of Death won't pay a visit to their homes and families as well, God instructs Moses how to spare the Hebrews from God's vengeance.

"God's word is clear—the blood of a firstborn lamb is his chosen sign," Moses lectures. "It is the sign that you are chosen people. Every single house must be marked with blood. Every one!"

Moses looks into the faces of his people, many of whom are holding their children tightly. Their faith in God is being tested to the breaking point.

Even Aaron is confused. "We promised that God would free our people. Yet now he sends death. How can this be?"

"We must trust in him," Moses whispers to Aaron.

Vengeance doesn't take long. The next morning, every firstborn son in Egypt is gone. Every last one. A dozen soldiers have arrived to tear Moses and Aaron from their beds.

"Leave them be," screams Miriam. "They've done nothing!"

But her words fall on deaf ears, and soon Aaron and Moses are being led through the towering palace doors.

Then they hear Rameses' voice. The sound of grief is unmistakable. "Why?" he cries. "Why should lowly Israelite slaves have life...when my son is dead? Is your God satisfied now?"

Moses and Aaron say nothing.

"I asked you a question."

Moses stays quiet. He only looks at Rameses with sadness, as if to remind him that all of this could have been prevented. If Rameses had only listened.

"Take your people and your flocks and go! Leave my land. And take your wretched God with you!" Rameses orders.

Moses and Aaron say nothing, eager to get out of the throne room as fast as possible.

Amid preparations for departure, people can't help but celebrate. The Hebrews seem to have permanent smiles on their faces, and they spontaneously sing and chant songs of joy. When it comes time to depart, Moses is carried through the city streets on the shoulders of men who were once wary of his presence. The impossible promise Moses made is coming true.

"Put me down!" Moses tells the group of men carrying him through a packed street. Children are running and jumping to get a better view of their new hero.

⁓

As the Israelites travel east out of Egypt, Rameses is having second thoughts.

Rameses pivots to his left, to where the captain of the guard stands watching along the wall. "We will bring them back," Rameses orders. "I will lead the way, Commander. The Hebrews want freedom? They're free to choose: crawl back to me as slaves—or die. Get my chariot!" he roars. "We leave immediately."

⁓

The Hebrews reach the Red Sea after a week's journey. To be truly out of Egypt, and free from the Pharaoh's power, they must cross to the far shore, a distance of many miles. They have no boats. Swimming is out of the question. There is no other option but to trust in God.

Trouble is fast approaching from the west. Horses'

hooves pound the desert floor. The chariots and the lines of soldiers following close behind kick up considerable dust—so much that they can be seen from miles away.

"Horses!" Joshua screams. "Chariots!"

The Hebrews panic. They begin packing their belongings as quickly as they can.

Moses looks at them in dismay.

An exasperated Aaron comes to Moses' side. "This is hopeless, brother. What do we do?"

"Do not be afraid," Moses commands.

Moses plants his feet in the sand and sinks his staff into the ground. The surf washes over his feet. Moses closes his eyes and lowers his head until it comes to rest on the staff. Moses shuts out the chaos and panic surrounding him.

Moses prays. "God, we need you now. Your people need you."

He remembers the moment when God appeared to him and told him the specific route he must follow to the Promised Land. Moses knows that he has done just as God commanded, so even as he prays, his faith is strong that God will find a way to deliver the Hebrews from this coming evil.

The sky is growing black, and a hard wind whips at his robe, sending his long hair flailing about his shoulders. "Lord, I know you have a plan for us. And I believe in your plan. And I believe that this is not the end you planned for us."

The strong wind whips up clouds of sand.

But Moses sees none of it. His faith is in God, and he continues to pray. "We have watched you bring terror on our enemies...."

The long line of chariots races down the road to the beach.

Moses' hand grips his staff ever tighter. "You kept death from our doors...."

Then Moses' eyes suddenly open as God speaks back to him. "Lord!" Moses says in shock.

The wind is now almost at hurricane strength. A funnel cloud touches down on the sea before Moses, hitting the water and then exploding back up into the sky.

Only Moses is left standing, not letting go of his staff as he raises his face to the heavens.

Before him, the sea rises to the sky, a great wall of water stretching from the earth to the clouds. All around him, the Israelites shield their eyes from the mist and spray, stunned at the vast wall of water climbing higher and higher right before their very eyes.

And then the water parts in two, forming a great

canyon. The seafloor is completely exposed, with water on either side. The wind rages through the gap.

Moses knows precisely what to do next. "Follow me," he cries, thrusting his staff into the sky. "This is God's work."

Aaron leaps to his feet and organizes the Israelites, hurrying them into the divide in the seas. They scramble toward the entrance, so eager to be safe from Pharaoh that many leave all their belongings behind. As they step inside, faces glance up in awe at the vast mountains of water. Ahead, there is darkness, and Joshua quickly orders the people to light torches. Moses leads the way, in silt and mud up to his ankles. Water from the parted sea drips in the smallest of droplets onto his head. The way is misty, loud, and dark, yet Moses presses on.

"Come on," Aaron encourages the Israelites. "Come quickly."

Joshua joins in, when he sees that the people are terrified of taking that first step of faith into the parted sea. "It's safe. Have faith," he cries.

Back on shore, some of the Egyptian horses balk at entering the watery tunnel. The Egyptian commanders order their men to dismount and grab their weapons. They stumble into the great chasm, their eyes adjusting to the darkness, even as they stumble over the rocky slime in their search for the Hebrews.

Moses trudges over sand and rocks. Ahead, he can see something new and quite miraculous: the sun. It is merely a faint disk right now, burning through the wall of mist. But the mist soon begins to part, and the sun burns brighter and brighter.

Joshua breaks ranks and charges toward it, a broad smile spreading across his face. "We're almost there! Come on!" he yells.

The light increases as the ground becomes total desert again. In ones and twos, the Israelites finally step onto the sand of safety. Then by tens and twenties. And then by the hundreds and thousands.

Now Moses turns around and faces the sea once more. Yet again he raises his staff to the sky. In the depths of the tunnel, he sees Pharaoh's army rushing forward.

The darkness is intense, but there is light on the faces of the Egyptians. Then they feel another sensation: drops of water. But this is not rain. The Egyptians glance up to the sky, just in time to see the great walls of water collapsing down onto them.

From the shore, the Israelites stand in stunned silence as they watch the ocean descend from the sky and drown Pharaoh's army. A great whoosh of wind is shoved from the chasm as it closes shut, but then the seas and the skies are calm.

"Thank you, Lord," shouts Joshua. "We are free at last."

∽

Moses tells the jubilant Israelites, "Come. There is a long road ahead. We must be strong." Their faith in God is enduring, and they will follow Moses anywhere God tells him to go. Thus begins forty years of wandering for the Israelites, in search of the land that God promised to give Abraham and his people.

God does more than lead them through the great desert wilderness; he gives Moses a set of rules to govern their lives. Moses returns alone to Mount Sinai, where he once tended his flock. There he receives the Ten Commandments, a moral code written in stone.

Moses descends Mount Sinai, carrying two stone tablets, and is greeted by Joshua. These will be placed inside the Ark of the Covenant, a sacred vessel, and carried by the Hebrews as their most holy possession. "God has renewed the promise he made to Abraham," Moses says, brimming with a faith greater than ever before. "We must worship no other God... no more lying...stealing...cheating...no more murder or dishonor...If we are true to God, he will keep his promise."

"Abraham's dream. That is our future?" asks Joshua.

"*You* are the Israelites' future now, Joshua. Don't look back. You must take the land promised to Abraham. And to all his descendants—as numerous as the stars."

PART THREE

DEFENDING THE HOMELAND

Jericho is an ancient city, settled time and again over the centuries by different cultures. Tall, thick walls that have kept out many an enemy surround it. The Hebrews have crossed into the Promised Land, and this cherished settlement calls to them. For forty years since escaping Pharaoh, the Israelites have wandered the wilderness of the desert. They have brought with them the Ark of the Covenant. Their Ark needs a home, as do they. And they are prepared to fight for it. Joshua has sent spies into the city to search for weaknesses.

"Joshua," exclaims a breathless Nashon as he races to their leader.

Joshua is hunkered down over a fire, breathing in the still night air and wondering how God will choose to get them inside the city.

"Tell me," asks Joshua, "did you find a way in? Is there a weakness?"

"The walls are solid and thick," Nashon exclaims. "But the people's hearts are not. We met a woman. She thinks that God has already taken the city and that there is nothing the people of Jericho can do about it. Their people are already melting in fear because they believe God is with us."

Joshua could leap for joy. "He is with us! But we've still got to find a way to get inside those walls."

Joshua claps Nashon on the shoulder and wanders away from the fire. He thinks of his old friend, long since departed, and his constant demonstrations of faith. "Moses, old friend," Joshua wonders aloud, "what would you do?"

As he saw Moses do so many times, Joshua climbs a nearby mountain. Then he falls to his knees and prays. This, he remembers, is what Moses did constantly: pray. When life was uncertain, Moses prayed for guidance. When life was spectacular, Moses prayed words of thanks. When life was mysterious, Moses prayed for wisdom. Prayer was Moses' way.

"Lord," he begins, "I was a slave when you showed me your love and your power....You gave me a new life, a life that I cherish, despite its daily hardships. You have brought us so far, but now these mighty city walls stand before us. What is your will? What would you have us do?"

Out of the silence comes a whoosh of air. The flames of Joshua's torch burn sideways as a blast of wind levels them. A great and mighty warrior has appeared out of nowhere and stands before him now. A hood covers his head, but nothing hides his posture, strong shoulders, and the great sword in his hand.

Joshua is terrified. "Who are you?" he asks very carefully.

The warrior is silent.

Joshua bows his head, overwhelmed. This warrior is mighty. Joshua slowly looks up and asks, "Are you with us or against us?"

The warrior's face is dark, and his eyes unblinking. "I am with God," he tells Joshua. There is no affect to his voice, just power. "I am commander of the Lord's army."

This is an answer to Joshua's prayer. As terrifying as the warrior might be, Joshua knows God is with him. "What does God ask of us?"

"The Lord parted the water for Moses—but for you..." The angel thrusts the blade of that great sword deep into the ground. Instantly, the earth begins to crack. The fissure widens and widens, spreading out around Joshua but never harming him. "He will split rock. This is what you must do...."

Joshua listens closely to what the angel tells him. Very closely.

⸻

It is daytime. The Israelite army assembles into an orderly formation and marches on Jericho. But they do not attack. Instead, they march around the city's walls, just as the commander of God's army ordered Joshua. They will repeat this exercise each day for six consecutive days, as instructed.

Joshua marches with his army, the words of the angel ringing in his ears:

"March around the city once a day with all the armed men. Do this for six days. Carry the Ark of the Covenant around the city. It contains God's commandments, showing that the Almighty is with you."

Joshua sees the men carrying the Ark. Thousands of sandal-covered feet kick up dust. *Yes*, he thinks, *we are doing precisely as I was told.*

But Joshua also knows that the best is yet to come. For on the seventh day, his men will not rest, as God did when creating the heavens and the earth. No, the

Israelite army will march seven times around the city walls, after which Israelite priests will blow a special trumpet made from the hollowed horn of a ram—called a shofar—and then, with an enormous shout from the Israelite army, the mighty walls of Jericho will fall down.

Joshua knows that up and down the ranks, many of his soldiers are struggling with this plan. It seems ludicrous, and most definitely impossible. To march around Jericho in the hot desert sun, clad in battle armor and coated in the thick clouds of dust produced by an army on the march, is the height of discomfort with no chance for valor. There is a great deal of grumbling, and Joshua knows that if this plan fails, his authority will be in question.

But he follows the plan and does not fear. Joshua has seen for himself what happens when a man has the faith to listen to God and do as instructed. He possesses that faith in great abundance. He marches, his mouth dry from the heat, ignores the cool shade of his tent calling to him, and waits eagerly for the seventh day.

When it does arrive, Joshua doesn't even wait for daylight to begin the seven laps around Jericho. The Israelites march by torchlight; the Ark of the Covenant is being carried by the strongest of their men, for its weight is considerable. Great expectation is palpable in the ranks, for after their forty years of waiting and wandering, God has promised them a home in this land. The Hebrews dream of solid roofs over their heads, and homes where they can raise their families in comfort and cleanliness.

One lap. Two. Jericho is large. Each circuit around its walls is a minor act of endurance. Four. Five. Men wonder if this far-fetched plan of Joshua's will work. He says it comes from God, and they believe him. But what if the walls don't fall? Will they still attack? Men wonder if this is the day they will die, and with that curiosity comes fear. They think of their loved ones, wondering if they will ever see them again. Jericho's army stands ready in the battlements atop the city walls with spears, swords, and battle-axes.

Six. Seven. A Hebrew commander holds up a hand to end the march. The men know what to do next, standing still as seven Israelite priests step forth and, in unison, press the shofars to their lips. As one, they sound a long blast.

This is the signal Joshua and his army have been waiting for. The entire Israelite army shouts as loudly as possible. The roar of the troops builds as the forty years of wilderness floods out of them. Joshua joins them, tilting his head back and letting loose a primal scream, shouting with all his heart and soul, remembering the words of the angel: "Glory will come."

Suddenly, Jericho's soldiers are hit by a shock wave. Their faces distort under the impact of the roaring sound. They fall backward off the walls and crash into the streets below. The noise floods over the walls and into the streets. The entire city is in chaos.

A bolt of lightning sizzles down from the black sky. A massive storm swirls overhead and a violent thunder rises from the desert floor. The earth begins to shake. The tremors are small at first, and then grow stronger and more violent.

The city walls have collapsed into rubble.

Then, almost as quickly as it began, the trembling stops.

The voice of Joshua cries out to his army. Without their walls to protect them, all of Jericho hears the words of Joshua ring out: "Jericho is ours! Every man must go in. We give this city to the Lord."

Joshua holds his arms to heaven. "God has kept his promise," he mutters joyfully to himself. "God has kept his promise." The former slave is now master of the Promised Land. His first thought is to give thanks, for he knows that God cherishes a thankful heart.

"Lord," he screams to his maker. His heart fills with gratitude and love for God. "Thank you."

Then Joshua hears it, a low and rumbling chant that spreads through Jericho. The words remind him of those days so long ago in Egypt, and the distant dream that someday the Israelite slaves would escape that awful world of toil and strife to create a home all their own. The chant is this: "Is-ra-el! Is-ra-el!" and it emanates from the lips of every Israelite soldier standing in the ruins of Jericho. Some are cheering. Some are crying tears of joy and exhaustion. From slaves to a nation. The impossible dream has become a reality: the Israelites are home.

"When we obey the Lord," Joshua tells anyone who will listen, "anything is possible."

Joshua is a man of faith. And for the next fifty years he leads the Israelite army as they conquer the Promised Land. He forges an Israelite nation built upon the ideal of each man and woman putting their hopes and dreams in the capable hands of God.

But when Joshua dies, that faith seems to die with him. Generations of Israelites forget their covenant with the Lord, turning to other gods to meet their needs—gods of rain and fertility, gods of the previous inhabitants of the Promised Land.

God is grieved by this betrayal. He reminds the Israelites of the covenant with Abraham, and that the

Promised Land is a gift that must be cherished. God uses hard, powerful armies to attack the Israelites, as a father disciplines his son.

The cycle will be repeated for hundreds of years: the Israelites break their covenant; God sends foreign armies to oppress them; they learn the lesson and cry out for help; God then raises a deliverer or "judge" to save them; and, once again, the land enjoys peace, until a future generation forgets God.

The Philistines are more powerful than all the foreign enemies that have subdued the rebellious Israelites to this point in history. They soon conquer the Israelites and claim much of the Promised Land for themselves. Yet God has not deserted his chosen people. He longs to renew his covenant with the Israelites and return to them the Promised Land.

It is 150 years since the death of Joshua. The Philistines control the coastal regions of the Promised Land. Despite being oppressed by them, some Israelites find their ways appealing. Some have even stopped worshipping the God of Abraham and instead choose to bow down to Philistine gods.

One day, an angel of the Lord appears to a woman

as she draws water from the village well. Though she prays daily for a child, her faith has not been rewarded.

"Do not be afraid," he tells her. "God will give you a son."

She is speechless as the angel suddenly disappears from her sight.

Then he stands behind her and informs her that there are conditions to this childbirth: "See to it that when your son is born, no razor may be used on his head. This will be the sign that the boy is given to God."

Unable to find words, she nods in agreement.

The boy is soon born and given the name Samson. By the age of eight, he knows the story of the angel by heart. His mother believes that he is destined to free the Israelites from the Philistines.

Ten years pass. Samson is a young man now, with a thick head of hair that flows in great, powerful locks, just as the angel requested. He is renowned for his feats of strength, like killing a lion with his bare hands. Some say there is no more powerful man in all of Israel. But Samson does nothing to free the Israelites from Philistine rule. That is, until one of them murders his wife.

The first to feel Samson's wrath is a Philistine guard standing watch near an alley. Unable to control his rage, Samson bursts into the barracks housing Philistine soldiers, brandishing a wooden club. He is instantly attacked by a half-dozen armed men, but he swats them away. Soldiers are thrown over the balcony into the courtyard below, and then Samson moves into the jail, opening the cells to release their Israelite prisoners. Just as on that great day when Joshua and the Israelite army laid waste to Jericho, Samson kills every Philistine in sight before storming into the night.

A shadow falls across the entrance to a cave situated high atop a steep cliff far outside town. A frightening and precarious path leads to this cave. Samson's aging mother now bravely makes the climb, accompanied by an elder named Elan and a small crowd of Israelites. They make their way upward, breathing hard from the effort, and take care not to look back down to the valley floor. Small rocks clatter down the slope from above, causing them to press their bodies into the face to avoid being hit.

At last, they reach the cave.

Samson's mother calls out, "Samson? Are you there, son?"

"Mother," Samson says as he emerges from the shadows. He towers over the Israelites, who now back away from him in fear. The depth of Samson's grief shows on his lined and weary face. There is a wild look to his eyes, and in the confines of the small cave Samson looks even more imposing than ever before. His long, thick hair rolls down onto his shoulders like a mane. He looks capable of killing every man, woman, and child in the land to avenge his wife.

"You must stop the killing, Samson. Please—for the sake of us all. For every Philistine you kill, two more appear, seeking revenge—on us," says Elan.

"As they did to me, so I have done to them."

Elan is growing exasperated. "Don't you realize that the Philistines are our rulers now?"

"Everyone," Samson replies, "must do what he thinks is right."

"No, Samson. Do what's right for your people and for God. Not for yourself."

Samson's mother steps forward and takes his hand.

"You must give yourself up, my son," she whispers tenderly.

"Is that what God wants?" replies a crushed Samson.

"Sometimes…you must trust in God. He leads us in ways we cannot see. He will guide the choices you make. We must trust in God."

Samson looks to the sky. It feels like an eternity. Then he bows his head and extends his powerful hands. With great relief, Elan nods, and two men step forward to bind those thick wrists with rope. Samson looks to his mother for support, but she cannot meet his eyes. Samson, the strongest man in the land, allows himself to be meekly led away.

Samson is now chained to a stone wall in the market square. Those powerful arms are secured straight out to each side, and the metal chains bite into his wrists. More than one man wonders if Samson will somehow break those chains and continue his revenge.

Only Abimilech, a Philistine commander, dares to come face-to-face with Samson. The two men stand inches apart, glaring into each other's eyes.

"Now that you have me, will you finally leave my people alone?" asks Samson.

Abimilech laughs. "Not until we drive you all back into the wilderness, where you belong."

The Philistine soldiers draw their swords. Abimilech steps back to watch.

Samson hears a voice. "Lord?" he replies, startled to realize that God has waited until his moment of greatest need to speak to him. Samson gazes at the ground, where the jawbone of a donkey rests in the desert dust, dirty and neglected. A new power ripples through Samson, and he knows that the bone has been placed there for a purpose. The soldiers are mere steps away. Samson is not looking at them, much to the dismay of Abimilech. Instead, Samson stares at the jawbone and speaks to God. "Lord," he asks more loudly, "is that you?"

"It is."

Samson hears God's voice and is amazed at the power beyond all power coursing through his muscles. Samson snaps his chains as if they were made of twigs. He takes hold of the steel links and swings them around his head to force the soldiers back. Believing that their sharpened swords will save them, the Philistines rush at him, only to have Samson drive them to the ground with the snap of a chain.

Samson then snatches the jawbone from the ground. Chains still dangle from his wrists, but now he has a weapon—a length of sun-dried bone no different from any other donkey's jawbone, but Samson wields it like the greatest weapon known to mankind.

After overtaking the Philistine soldiers, Samson doesn't walk far. The moment he turns a corner into an alley, he falls to his knees. Breathlessly, he presses his hands together and speaks to God. "Lord," he asks, "is this what you want? Please, I beg of you, guide me."

Samson hears footsteps behind him. He leaps to his feet, jawbone in hand, believing it to be yet another soldier. But it is a woman. She is clearly a Philistine, but she is so utterly stunning that Samson forgets his rage and simply stares into her dark eyes. The woman carries a jug of water, which she now places on the ground. Staring into Samson's eyes, she pulls back the scarf that covers her head, then bends to pour a cup of water and holds it up for him to drink.

Samson suddenly realizes his great thirst. Hours chained in the market square have made him parched. He feels the thickness of his tongue, and his lips are dry, chapped. He drinks greedily.

Samson gulps the last of the water and wipes his lips with the back of his hand. "Who are you?" he says finally.

"My name is Delilah," she answers.

⁓

Time passes and Samson grows to trust Delilah. But this is dangerous. Abimilech has offered Delilah thousands of silver coins to find out the truth behind Samson's strength.

"You seem invincible," she says innocently one day. "Can anyone defeat you?"

A confused Samson turns to face her. "What do you mean?"

"Just curious. There seems to be a secret to your strength. If we are to be together, we shouldn't have secrets."

"God is with me, Delilah," he finally answers. "He makes me strong."

"But how? How does he make you strong?"

"My hair. I have never cut my hair. I'm forbidden. It's my sign of devotion. If I cut my hair, my God will take away my strength."

Samson can't help but smile.

"You don't believe me, do you?" he says.

Delilah smiles back.

"I do, Samson," she replies. "I believe you completely."

Samson stirs but doesn't awaken at the first snip as Delilah takes shears to his hair. She is cautious, starting at the longest end, far away from his head. But his hair is so long that it is as if she has cut nothing at all. Another snip. And then another. Soon it is gone—all of it. And still, he sleeps. The final lock falls to the floor just as Philistine soldiers rush into the room.

"Take him!" Abimilech orders.

In that instant Samson is up on his feet and ready to fight. He touches a hand to his head and feels the stubble. He sees a pile of dark hair and looks at Delilah, only to have her turn away. His heart sinks. The Philistine soldiers easily hold him down. Samson fights back, but he has no strength at all. For the first time in his life, Samson is weak and afraid. "What have you done?" he yells to Delilah.

Abimilech empties the box of silver coins onto the bed, where they mingle with the coils of hair like exotic jewelry.

Samson's eyes dart to Delilah. He is dumbfounded by her betrayal and curses his own foolishness.

Samson has been chained up in prison for months and has gone blind. His hair has grown longer and longer.

Samson presses his forehead against the cool stone. He is alone, his eyes covered in bandages. Darkness is his world. But it is in this darkness that he finally begins to see that his destiny will be fulfilled. Behind him, the door creaks as it swings open.

Two Philistine soldiers pummel him with fists and clubs, taking great delight in their work. Samson roars in pain as the blows rain against his body, and his chains make a great clanking noise as he waves his arms in a futile attempt to protect himself. But with his strength and sight gone, there is nothing Samson can do.

Only when Samson sags forward against the chains, unable to support his own body weight, do the soldiers unchain him, continuing their kicks and punches as the key turns in the locked manacles around his wrists and ankles.

When Samson collapses, they drag him from the cell into the temple of the Philistine god Dagon. The room is packed with hundreds of people. Incense smoke wafts over their faces, and their eyes are watery and bloodshot. Pigs are being roasted. Goblets of wine are filled and refilled. Dogs are allowed inside this great pagan assembly, and their barks and howls ricochet off the tall stone pillars supporting the roof.

"Samson, Samson, Samson," they chant as his body is dragged through their throng.

When the Philistine soldiers release Samson, he rises to his feet, confused. Samson hears the ridicule, yet he cannot see who is showering him with oaths and profanities. He senses Delilah's presence in the room and turns in her direction.

Samson falters, on the verge of passing out once more. "I'm weak," he cries. "Stand me up against something."

The guards lead Samson to the building's central pillars.

"Lord God," he whispers, "if I am yours, remember me and strengthen me once more so that I may have my revenge."

Abimilech overhears Samson's prayer and leans his face close to Samson's. "Haven't you forgotten, Samson? You have broken your pact with your God, and now he has abandoned you."

Samson leans hard into the pillar, suddenly pushing on it with all his might. He closes his eyes and prays a last prayer to God. "Lord, remember me. Please, God, strengthen me."

Abimilech shakes his head as he watches Samson pray. "It's over, Samson. Don't you see that?"

But then something hard slaps Abimilech's hand.

He looks down and sees shards of fine stone. Then a cloud of dust seems to lower itself from the ceiling. A disbelieving Abimilech swivels his view back to Samson leaning against the pillar. His muscles ripple with their former strength.

Then Abimilech realizes the truth: Samson's hair has grown back, but it was never the entire source of his power. It comes from God. Those great locks were just a reminder of Samson's pact.

The power comes from God. The God of the Israelites. And it always has.

Screams echo through the chamber. Philistine guards throw themselves at Samson, desperate to pull him from the pillar, but he swats them away as the roof begins to cave and great sections fall to the floor.

Samson finishes what he started. The pillar topples, and finally Samson can stop pushing. He stands and smiles, nearly invisible in the dust and ruin. All around him the temple is collapsing, and he knows that his time has come.

But Samson's victory is short-lived. The Philistines continue to wage war on the Israelite people.

It has been many years since the God of Abraham

has spoken to his people, when he sends them a prophet. Samuel, whose name means "he hears God," turns to God to wage war against the Philistines. He leads the Israelites to many great successes. God will reveal the future of the Israelites to this man. Not only will he deliver the Israelites from the Philistines, but he will also become their greatest spiritual leader since Moses.

Now well over fifty, Samuel gathers with the elders and priests at his home.

Phinehas, an elder, speaks for the group. "We are grateful, prophet. You have given us great victories."

"God has given us great victories," Samuel corrects him.

"But who will speak to the Lord after you are gone?"

"Tell me: what do our people want? What will reassure them that God will hear their cries?"

Phinehas speaks just two words: "A king."

Samuel is dumbfounded. "A king? This is a most dangerous idea. God is our king."

"Why should we be different from other nations?" demands Phinehas.

"But look what other nations' kings have done to their people. Kings become tyrants. They enslave their own kind," Samuel shouts.

"But never in history has a king been anointed by a prophet of God. That king would be different."

"God has promised us this land," Samuel argues. "It is not right for one of us to become king."

"How do we know that, Samuel?" counters Phinehas. "Have you asked him?"

Samuel is alone atop a desert hill. His thoughts are focused on God. Their partnership has molded the Israelite people ever since the death of Samson. In the many dreams and conversations in which God has revealed his plans, there has never once been mention of an earthly king. So this idea put forth by the elders—an idea that has great merit—is stupefying. Is this an idea of man's or of God's? Samuel needs to know the answer.

"I have given everything," he explains to God. "But if you say I should give them a king, of course I will. But what should I do?"

God tells Samuel that they are not rejecting Samuel when they ask for a king. They are, instead, rejecting God. He tells Samuel to warn the people that an earthly king will be corrupt and they will be very sorry when they live under the pain he causes them. But despite God's and Samuel's warnings, the people demand a king, so God decides to answer their prayers and give them one.

God plants an image in Samuel's head. It is that of a man who is physically head and shoulders above everyone else. Good with a sword and at home on the field of battle: Saul.

Samuel bows his head. Then an idea hits him. He looks up at the darkening skies. "He will be the king and I will still be your prophet, O Lord. I can guide your king."

Samuel goes in search of Saul, to name him the first king of Israel. He finds him weeks later, in a small village. Before a crowd of hundreds who chant his name in adulation, Saul is proclaimed the Israelite ruler. Samuel anoints the new king with oil, and the Holy Spirit comes upon him.

It does not take long for Saul to lead the Israelites into battle. On the morning of one planned attack, Saul and a small band of soldiers crouch low and run up a slope that overlooks an encampment of the enemy. Saul has been told by Samuel to wait seven days, at which time Samuel will come and make the required sacrifice to God. Those seven days have almost passed.

"Are the men ready?" he says in a level voice to a nearby officer.

"Yes," comes the reply.

"And Samuel," Saul asks. "Any sign? We must make a sacrifice before we strike."

The officer takes a breath and shakes his head.

There has been no sign, no message, nothing at all to let Saul know Samuel's whereabouts or plans. This is the first test of their uneasy partnership. Saul feels abandoned. There is no longer time to wait. His men are growing impatient. Saul is losing his confidence. There must be a sacrifice before battle. In his impatience and presumption, he believes Samuel won't come, so he takes Samuel's place as priest and prophet and performs the sacrifice himself.

Suddenly, a voice can be heard shouting angrily at Saul. "May God forgive you," cries Samuel. "May God forgive you!"

Saul looks up to see Samuel striding up the hill toward him, pushing his way through a thick crowd of impatient soldiers. "Where were you?" cries a furious Saul. "Seven days we've been waiting. My men are deserting."

"Focus on being a military leader," Samuel orders. "And leave the job of being a priest to me. God will not honor your sacrifice."

"I don't have time to argue, Samuel. Some of us have a fight to win. Some of us might not return."

"Remember, God instructs you to destroy everything in this battle you are about to wage. Do not spare anyone."

Saul then orders his men to assemble.

The attack goes according to plan. After a week of waiting, the entire battle takes just ten minutes. His men have even taken a battle-scarred warrior prisoner, and they lead him to a small wooden cage.

Saul has won his first victory since becoming king. "God is with me," he shouts, thrusting his arms to the heavens. "God is with me."

His men cheer Saul as they round up the goats and cattle captured from the enemy. The Israelites have eaten little in the past few weeks, and the prospect of a hot meal does wonders for morale.

Samuel watches from atop a nearby ridge. He has seen the battle and hears Saul's delighted cries. "Are you really with him, Lord?" Samuel asks. "Really?"

The prisoner is alive. And so are the best of his herds of cattle and goats. Yet Samuel told Saul that God specifically ordered him to destroy everything in the village. Now, as the evening campfires roar, Samuel confronts Saul in front of his army. "You had one task. One simple command from God. And what was that?"

"I have done what God commanded," replies a seething Saul.

"Your descendants could have ruled for a thousand years, but because of your actions today, God has forsaken you."

Saul grabs Samuel as he turns away. The fabric of his robe tears off in Saul's clenched fist. Rather than be outraged, Samuel quickly seizes the opportunity to make a point.

"Just as you have torn my robe, so God has torn your power from you. He wants a man after his own heart."

Saul storms away, muttering under his breath about Samuel's arrogance. Back in his tent, he stares hard at the scrap of fabric in his hands. "Perhaps I was too hasty," he says, shaking his head. "Perhaps I should ask Samuel's forgiveness."

Saul calls to his servant. "Bring Samuel to me," he orders.

"He's gone, Highness," replies the servant.

Saul storms out, screaming for Samuel, but the prophet is long gone—gone to find a new king.

PART FOUR

A Man After
God's Own Heart

Saul remains Israel's king for now. He knows nothing of Samuel's whereabouts or actions. It is the end of yet another battle in the midst of the endless, arid desert of the Promised Land. Once again, Saul's army has won, for he has no equal in waging war. Although he is outnumbered, he continues to defeat the Philistines, Israel's most feared enemy.

Despite his victories, he still stings from his final confrontation with Samuel. And the question, that infernal question, constantly nags at him: *has God turned his back on me?*

Saul's sleep is not restful. It never is. It's been years since Samuel left, and he has since died. But Saul's fear that he disobeyed God haunts him each and every time he closes his eyes. In his dreams, he relives that long-ago battle. He winces at the memory of ignoring Samuel. Saul's impatience—his insistence on not waiting those seven full days, and his offering sacrifice himself before Samuel could arrive—haunts him. He was so youthful then, so callow, so eager for his first battle to be won.

Night after night, Saul dreams of how he would do it all differently if he had the chance. He would wait those seven days and listen closely to Samuel as he shared God's word and then performed the sacrifice. Saul would not just run roughshod over the field of battle; he would swing his great sword like an avenging angel.

Alone in his tent, Saul cries out in his sleep. "No... no...Lord, please, I beg of you: forgive your servant." But he knows what's done is done. Saul has been forgiven, but he must still bear the consequences of his disobedience.

Saul eagerly straps on his battle armor with the help of a young armor bearer named David. His army is camped in the Valley of Elah, already drawn up in battle array to face the Philistines yet again, and Saul couldn't be happier. He is excited at the thought of the action.

Suddenly, a breathless Jonathan, one of Saul's sons,

throws back the flap and steps into his tent. "Father, you must come immediately!"

David trails behind as Saul pushes his way through the Israelite troops. Looking down into the valley, they see a man almost nine feet tall standing alone, facing Saul's army. He wears full armor and wields a sword that matches his immense physical size. The entire Philistine army stands behind him.

"Israelites," calls out the giant. "I am Goliath. And I have a proposition for you!"

Saul peers down intently, unsure of what he will hear next.

"Send just one of you to fight me, oh Israelites. Just one. If he wins, then we Philistines will be your slaves. But if I win, you will be our slaves."

When he receives no response from Saul or the other Israelites, Goliath continues his rant. "Come now," he goads them. "Surely there is one of you courageous enough to fight me."

"I'll do it!" The calm, sure voice of a boy cuts across the valley, answering Goliath's call. It is David. He is a seventeen-year-old shepherd, accomplished at playing the harp, and a part-time armor bearer for Saul. He has never once stepped onto the field of battle.

Saul gives him a patronizing smile. "David, the

reward would be great, but you're not a soldier. You're a shepherd."

"Yes," David replies, catching Saul's eye before the king can look away. "And I've protected my sheep from wolves. Just as I've protected my sheep, so God will protect me."

Saul is not swayed, even though Goliath has ratcheted up the tone of his chants, until he is now insulting not just the Israelites but God, too.

"Where is your faith?" chants Goliath. "Where is your God?"

The Israelites continue to cower. But David has deep faith, and Goliath's words stir his anger.

The final straw comes with Goliath's next taunt: "I don't believe that your God is on your side at all. Your God is not as strong as our gods." He beams broadly toward the Philistines, who resume the beating of their shields.

"What will be done for the man who kills this Philistine and removes his disgracer from Israel?" David asks the nearby Israelite soldiers. "Who is this Philistine that he should defy the armies of the living God?"

He does not ask Saul's permission as he gathers his stones and weaves through the Israelite ranks, each step taking him closer and closer to the valley floor. David is just a teenager, but Saul is impressed. He quickly removes his battle armor and has it hand-carried down to David. But the armor is far too big for the shepherd to wear. He takes it off and heads into battle with just his sling.

"Go," Saul calls after him. "And the Lord be with you."

David emerges from the front of the Israelite line and squares off against Goliath, a grown man and battle-scarred veteran nearly three feet taller than he. David's quiet prayers escalate as the reality of what he has done—and is about to do—threaten to overwhelm him. "Yea, though I walk through the valley of the shadow of death, I will fear no evil. For you are with me. Your rod and staff...they comfort me. You anoint my head with oil. My cup overflows. Surely goodness and mercy will follow me all the days of my life."

Goliath raises a hand to silence the shield beating as David plants his feet and squarely presents himself. David's heart hammers inside his chest. Goliath roars a giant-sized laugh. "Is this Israel's champion?" he bellows, barely able to contain his glee.

David says nothing. He reaches into his satchel, never once taking his eye off Goliath.

"Don't waste my time, little boy," yells Goliath.

"You come against me with sword and spear, but I

come against you in the name of the Lord Almighty, whom you have defied."

The giant draws his sword and advances, his great strides eating up the distance all too quickly.

David stays calm. He pulls a stone from the bag on his belt and slips it into the cradle of his sling. "For you are with me," he prays. "Your rod and staff...they comfort me."

Goliath laughs as he sees David rotate the sling around and around his head. From above, Saul and Jonathan look on without hope, wishing one of them had felt confident enough to face the giant, as they consider their coming enslavement.

David's sling swings faster and faster around his head, the leather and rock whirring louder and louder. Goliath slashes at the air menacingly with his sword, not breaking stride as he bears down on David. Goliath turns to give yet another derisive sneer back toward his lines. But young David never once takes his eyes off Goliath.

As Goliath's head is turned ever so slightly, David lets the stone fly from his sling. That flat, smooth rock strikes the giant squarely on the temple, then falls harmlessly to the ground.

Goliath doesn't know what has happened. His eyes open wide in shock. He stands still.

Young David does not reload his sling. He merely stands, empty sling dangling from his side, and waits. Waits. Waits.

Then Goliath falls, just as David knew he would. A cloud of dust billows up from the earth, which seems to rumble as Goliath's massive form collides with the battlefield.

The Israelite army roars, even as the Philistines stare in horror.

Without waiting for a signal from their king, the Israelites charge onto the plain past David, racing forth with drawn swords and raised spears to lay waste to the Philistines.

David is triumphant. He beams as Saul approaches and claps him on the shoulder. "A wolf in sheep's clothing is what you are, David. You've saved my kingdom." Saul hands David a sword. "Come. We have an enemy to conquer."

The Philistines are the first of many enemies David will fight for Saul. As the years pass, David conquers all the enemies of Israel, always fighting alongside the man he calls his king. The Philistines are driven from the Promised Land, and David forges a deep bond of friendship with Saul and Jonathan. The Israelite army believes that David is invincible, and he soon becomes a great leader of men—a hero. He becomes so beloved by the Israelites that Saul, incredibly jealous, wishes him dead. What he doesn't know is that David has a secret. Before all this began, at a time when he was just the youngest of many brothers, the prophet Samuel personally anointed him to become king of the Jews.

David is on the run. Wherever he goes, Saul is just one step behind. The man who was made king to lead the Israelites against the Philistines is now distracted with hunting down David and anybody loyal to him. Saul and his men range far and wide across the broad deserts and valleys of the Promised Land, leaving a cruel wake of violence and mayhem.

At the end of a long day of chasing David, Saul's troops are encamped by a river. Tents are erected. Horses are being fed. Saul walks off from the camp. He is alone, and he likes it that way. At the base of a cliff he looks right and left to see if anyone can hear him, and then Saul cries out to the Lord. "I have served you faithfully," he says, "as faithfully as a man can. And still it seems it is not enough. Lord, I ask you, do you hear your servant?"

He waits, but there is silence. Nothing. He wearily walks on, looking for a cool, dry cave to get out of the heat. Finally, he finds one. Saul steps inside. He looks around, searching for signs of life—predatory animals, poisonous snakes, or perhaps a desert ruffian who has made the cave a home.

But he sees nothing, not even a hooded David standing behind a nearby rock.

David cries out, "Majesty!"

Saul spins around, recognizing the voice and drawing his sword. "David?"

David removes his hood from his head. "Why do you hunt me down? Why? I have done you no harm."

Saul warily approaches the shadows, sword at the ready. David steps toward him, and his soldiers follow. They draw their swords, but David uses one arm to wave them back.

"I could have killed you just now," David tells Saul.

"Why didn't you?" Saul asks.

"I will not kill you. Ever."

Saul considers what David has said. Then he sheathes his sword and looks chillingly into David's eyes as he holds out his hand. "Come, then...let's go home...together."

David is wary. He holds Saul's gaze, and as he does so his men tighten their grip on their swords. Showing grace and a quiet strength, he walks to Saul, shakes his head, bows, and then turns to join his men.

Saul, looking wretched and aged, turns and walks back alone to his camp.

Just an hour earlier he beseeched God to speak with him. And now he realizes that God has sent him a very clear message—though not the message that Saul longed to hear.

The dignity of the monarchy now belongs to David. He is the man who will be king. It's just a matter of time.

That night, Saul sits alone in his tent. Outside, he hears the thunder of hooves, signaling the arrival of a messenger. Then Jonathan enters, breathless.

"Father!" Jonathan cries.

"What is it, son?" growls Saul.

"The Philistine army is in the next valley. Near Gilboa—"

For once, Saul couldn't care less about battle. "Jonathan," he says gently, "David is near."

"Forget David! You must defend your kingdom. It is your duty!"

Saul feels a strange lack of confidence. "We leave at dawn," he mumbles meekly. "At dawn. Tell the men. And now leave me, son. I must seek guidance."

After Jonathan departs, Saul wanders alone into the night. He aims for the raging fire he has seen in the distance these past few evenings, for he knows that it is the camp of a pagan woman who speaks to the dead.

Saul is dazed, tormented. He would be easy prey if he were attacked during his journey, for he carries no sword and is incapable of defending himself. Finally, he sees the flames and hears the jangle of shells and bones that hang in a tree, blown by the wind. Saul makes a simple request: "Bring up the spirit of the dead prophet Samuel."

The woman does not make eye contact with Saul. Instead, the seer speaks to the flames: "We ask you... the dead...for an audience with the prophet Samuel."

Samuel appears to Saul, sitting on a rock right next to him. "Why? Why do you wake me? Why do you disturb my spirit?"

"F-f-forgive me," an astonished Saul stammers. "I only called you because...because when I speak to the Lord he does not answer."

Samuel looks bemused. "The Lord? Really?" A smile now flits across his bearded face. "You disobeyed the Lord," he reminds Saul.

"I tried to obey," Saul answers. "Really. I tried."

"He has torn your kingdom from you and given it

to David." Samuel glares at the man he once anointed king. "Look at me, Saul."

Saul doesn't want to. He doesn't know whether Samuel is real or a ghost. To look into Samuel's eyes is to look into some great abyss that Saul has never seen before. But he looks anyway.

"This battle will be your last," Samuel says evenly.

"No. Please. No."

"Soon you will be with me in the cold earth, Saul— as will your son."

"Take me," Saul begs. "But spare Jonathan."

But Samuel is gone. The only sound Saul hears is the rattle of bones and shells clanging in the wind.

When Samuel's prophecy comes true, and the Philistines kill Jonathan, Saul's spiral into despair is complete.

David and his men wait for the news from the fight. When word comes of Saul and Jonathan, he is devastated. Uriah, his trusted lieutenant and confidant, moves toward his friend. "You don't see it, do you?" asks Uriah.

David is puzzled. He has no answer.

"This is the beginning, David. Our time has come."

Now the other men spill out of the cave and walk toward David, realizing that the new ruler of Israel stands before them. "The people will look to you to defend them," Uriah tells his friend. "They will want you to unite the Israelites once again."

David stares at Uriah, taking in his words. They wash over him, soak into him, revitalize him. David grips Uriah's arm tightly and embraces him. "Thank you, dear friend. You are right. If God has cleared the way, we must be strong."

Now he looks at his men. He knows precisely what he must do next. "Let it begin," he pronounces.

Uriah pulls away from David's embrace. He looks David in the eye as an equal for the last time, and then slowly kneels. "Yes, my king. Let it begin."

The other men follow Uriah's lead, so that now David is the only man standing.

"King David!" they roar.

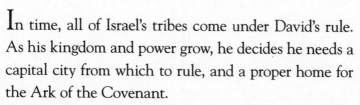

In time, all of Israel's tribes come under David's rule. As his kingdom and power grow, he decides he needs a capital city from which to rule, and a proper home for the Ark of the Covenant.

The city he chooses is just five miles from David's

childhood home in Bethlehem. It is an inspired choice, situated at the crossroads of the north and south trading routes, with deep valleys protecting it on three sides, and a constant supply of fresh water nearby.

David plans to conquer the city and give it a new name: City of David. Later it will be known as Jerusalem. It is a name that honors God, for it means "God is peace." The last part of the word is *shalom* in Hebrew.

In David's dream, he sees that Israel will finally know peace during his reign. That will one day come to pass.

This ancient fortress is already occupied by the Jebusites. If David is to make the city his own, he must take it by force. The king of Israel has a plan to penetrate enormous and guarded walls.

Nighttime. David's torso is wedged inside a sewer pipe. He emerges into a larger tunnel and lights a torch. Soon, the rest of his army climbs into the light behind him.

The men crawl slowly through the sludge. They do not speak, and communicate only by hand signals. The tunnel soon opens up into a wider chamber completely filled with deep water. Their way is blocked by iron bars rising from the ceiling and extending down into the depths below.

Uriah looks at David and raises an eyebrow. *What do we do next?* he seems to be asking.

David simply hands him his torch and dives into the filthy water. A minute passes. And then what seems like another. Uriah and the others anxiously watch and wait, peering down into the muck to where the bottom of the iron bars might be. It feels like an eternity.

Suddenly, David surfaces and treads water on the opposite side of the bars. "Come on."

Uriah hesitates. He's never been much of a swimmer, even in the clearest of waters. But to immerse himself in this filth and then open his eyes to find his way... the thought is repulsive. A glance at the other men shows that they are experiencing the same fears. "Leave the torches," David commands. With three simple words and a powerful tone of voice, he has reminded the men that he is no mere soldier. He is the king. And he must be obeyed. Uriah sets down his torch and jumps in. The quiet splashes of the other men soon follow.

A passage leads from the sewer into the city's underground reservoir, filled with drinking water. David and the men happily immerse themselves in the cool, clear water, eager to clean themselves. They swim onward through the cistern until a thin shaft of light plays on the water.

"A well," Uriah says with a smile.

David merely nods, his eyes searching the narrow stone walls for the one requirement vital to all wells: a rope. He spies it in the cleft between two rocks and swims for it.

Within ten minutes David and his men have all pulled themselves up the rope and out of the well. They are now inside the walled city of Jebus. They move quietly through the nighttime shadows. It is well past midnight, and the city is asleep.

Only when he and his men are in position does David yell his battle cry: "Israel!"

David stands on the roof, surveying a model of his proposed temple in front of him. The sight is beautiful to behold. It is broad daylight. From his palace's rooftop terrace, he can look down into the courtyards of the many homes and gardens that surround its walls.

A man clears his throat behind him. "Your Majesty?"

David turns to see the robed prophet Nathan strolling tentatively across the terrace.

"Ah, prophet!" David enthuses. "Look! My temple... for the Ark."

"I don't understand, Your Highness. You've summoned me to discuss...a temple?"

David beckons to him and points down to the small architectural model of his glorious temple. It is stunning to behold, with towering pillars and the sturdy walls of a fortress. "The world has never seen anything like this, prophet. The Lord will be pleased."

But if Nathan is dazzled, he does not show it. He stands still. Then he speaks in solemn tones. "The Lord came to me last night."

"And tell me: is he pleased with our work?"

"The Lord told me this: the House of David will rule over Israel forever."

"We are blessed," David exults, overcome with joy.

"Your son will be king," Nathan is telling him. "He will build this temple."

"My temple?"

"God's temple," Nathan corrects.

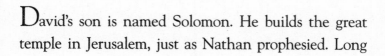

David's son is named Solomon. He builds the great temple in Jerusalem, just as Nathan prophesied. Long after his parents pass on, that temple provides a permanent home for the Ark of the Covenant.

Solomon gains a reputation as the wisest man in the world. His rule as king of Israel is a time of prosperity and peace. But Solomon is a man easily corrupted by his privilege and passions. After he dies, power continues to corrupt Israel's kings. Maintaining God's kingdom on earth becomes harder and harder as powerful new enemies emerge to threaten the Israelite claim to the Promised Land.

A new prophet named Daniel will have a dream in which God promised to once again save the Israelites by sending them a new king. But Daniel does not know when he will come. Nor does Daniel know that this king will be directly descended from David, nor that his name will be Jesus.

PART FIVE

SURVIVAL

It is three hundred years since the death of King Solomon. The Babylonian Empire has claimed a part of the Promised Land. King Zedekiah sits on the throne in Jerusalem, but his reign is one of fear and oppression. The religious leaders of Jerusalem have perverted the people, turning worship into an act of commerce and enriching themselves at the expense of the faithful. But time has passed, and Jerusalem is now under attack. Armies from the east have come and laid siege to the City of David, just as he once took it from the Jebusites.

As the sun rises, Jeremiah is hunched, his head and wrists locked in the wooden stocks. Though he is an old man, deserving of respect, people shout abuse as they walk past, and Jeremiah accepts it. This is his lot in life. Jeremiah knows he was marked as a prophet before he was even born.

But Jeremiah's will has finally been broken. He no longer has the strength to preach. His body aches each and every day from his many injuries. His head has been shoved to the ground and kicked more times than he can remember. He is alone. Always alone. God is his refuge and his solace. His comforter.

"They will never hear," Jeremiah mumbles. "If I cannot open their hearts with truth, and help them remember the Lord's compassion, what else is left?"

Jeremiah's prayers are answered by his one friend on earth: Baruch. The scribe hurries to the stocks, where he bribes the soldier standing guard to unlock the chains. The soldier is shocked to see a member of the royal court standing before him, wearing the brightly colored robes of his position. He takes the money and looks the other way.

"Why are you doing this?" Jeremiah asks as Baruch drags him away. "If they find out, you'll lose everything."

Baruch would not ordinarily put himself at such great risk, but God has moved him to act, putting it upon Baruch's heart to help Jeremiah. So as he comes to Jeremiah's aid, he says the words God placed so carefully on Baruch: "I can no longer remain silent. I've seen you before. I've heard you speak. And I've always known that God is with you."

Baruch pulls Jeremiah into a small room in the temple. Finding a cloth and bucket of water, he cleans the scum off Jeremiah's face.

Then Jeremiah begins channeling the words of God. "They have set up their detestable idols...defiled my house..."

Baruch is listening to the words of God, as God speaks them. He frantically hunts for a scroll to write it all down.

"Prepare yourself. I am bringing disaster from the north," Jeremiah continues. "I am bringing terrible destruction."

Baruch scribbles furiously.

"I will hand all your country over to my servant... the king of Babylon. I will make even the wild animals subject to him.

"I will lay waste to the towns of Judah so that no man can live there," Jeremiah channels. "I will make Jerusalem a heap of ruins, a haunt of jackals."

Hand shaking, heart pounding, Baruch writes down every word.

Jeremiah's prophecy comes true. King Nebuchadnezzar's enormous and terrifying Babylonian army has camped outside the walls of Jerusalem. It is too late to repent, and far too late to heed God's warnings.

When Zedekiah climbs to the highest room in his palace and looks out into the distance, he sees the Babylonian army preparing to lay siege to Jerusalem. Every day their numbers grow larger, and every day their force grows closer and closer to launching the great attack that will doom Zedekiah's kingdom.

Jeremiah is determined to deliver a harsh new message to Zedekiah—and in a way that the king will never forget. Jeremiah finds a wooden yoke, the type that is used to tether cattle. With Baruch's help, he hoists it onto his narrow shoulders and staggers into the palace. A stunned silence greets Jeremiah as he enters. The prophet looks preposterous, as if he will crumble under the weight of the yoke. But there is an undeniable fire in his eyes; no trace of fear or weakness is evident in Jeremiah's demeanor when he stands before the king.

"What is this?" snarls Zedekiah, angry that Jeremiah refuses to grovel before his king.

"This is you, as you will be under the yoke of Babylon."

"I will never succumb to Babylon," Zedekiah replies. "I called you here to speak to God on behalf of me and my kingdom."

Abraham places his faith in God.

King Nebuchadnezzar and his chariots invade Jerusalem.

The Babylonians bow to the Persian king
as he rides into the city with his men.

Daniel prays in secret.

The wise men journey to find the new king.

Joseph and Mary flee Bethlehem with the infant Jesus.

Jesus and the disciples spread his ministry.

They feed thousands of people with the loaves and fishes.

Jesus prays at the Last Supper.

Jesus is led to his trial.

Atop his stallion, Pontius Pilate prepares to enter Jerusalem.

A guard holds the crown of thorns.

Mary reaches out to her son.

Jeremiah continues as if he hasn't heard the king. "If you're wise, you will listen to what I have to tell you."

"And what is that?"

"Bow your neck and serve. Submit to Babylon and you will live."

One of Zedekiah's courtiers springs upon Jeremiah, throwing the yoke to the ground. "Wretch," says the courtier with utter disdain. "How dare you tell your king to bow his neck?"

Jeremiah doesn't flinch. His face flushes in anger as he squares off before his attacker. "No," answers Jeremiah. "How dare *you* question the words of your Lord God?"

One of the chief priests, thinking he will make points with Zedekiah, says, "You wrote that we should repent and all will be well. That God will be with us."

Jeremiah fixes the priests with a look of pity. He alone knows that Zedekiah's pride has already guaranteed Israel's fall. The Promised Land will now be Nebuchadnezzar's. Her people will be scattered and enslaved. Her temple will be destroyed. This is God's prophecy—this is as God allows. All the protestations of courtiers and high priests cannot stop this from happening.

"Look outside the walls. You're too late," says Jeremiah.

"Take him to the palace dungeon!" hisses Zedekiah.

Months pass. Inside the city, the people of Jerusalem are trapped and starving, deprived of food and much of their water supply by the Babylonian presence. Time has come for King Nebuchadnezzar to capture the city. Zedekiah's army tries to hold the gate, but they are disorganized and weak from hunger, and they cannot withstand the Babylonians.

Inside the palace, chaos reigns.

The dungeon has been emptied of all but one prisoner: Jeremiah.

Baruch makes his way through the empty palace. Its walls are lit by the burning city. The footsteps of his sandal-clad feet echo on the stone floor.

Baruch frees Jeremiah and ushers the prophet out of the palace. They race to the temple designed so long ago by David, cavernous, and usually a refuge of calm and tranquility. It is the spiritual home to God's covenant with the Israelites, where the Ark of the Covenant resides. It is about to burn to the ground. The few remaining faithful within the city are inside, working feverishly to save precious scrolls and religious artifacts. The Israelites hide the Ark of the Covenant in order to prevent it from being taken to Babylon.

Baruch and Jeremiah run from the temple, hoping to find a way to escape the city. They turn and take one last look back at the great building, its rooftop now licked by flames. Smoke billows into the sky. Screaming people fill the streets, soon to be taken to Babylon as slaves.

This is what the end of the Promised Land looks like.

Just as Jeremiah prophesied.

Years pass. After conquering Arabia, Egypt, and what will become Europe, King Nebuchadnezzar returns to Babylon to enjoy the wealth and spoils of his vast kingdom. His subjects slowly and reluctantly adapt to their ruler and his ways. Generations of children are brought into the world and grow to adulthood never knowing any difference between Nebuchadnezzar's customs and those of their forefathers. The Israelites unwittingly join in the worship of their king's pagan idols, having long lost even the memory of the God of Abraham.

Those who do remember feel God has forsaken them. Most don't know who God is at all.

However, one Israelite in exile—Daniel—has been blessed in a strange and powerful way. He has a God-given gift to interpret dreams.

This gift comes with a certain peril, though. For once Nebuchadnezzar learns of Daniel's special ability to listen and hear God in all circumstances, the king inquires about the meaning of his own dreams.

On a spectacular morning, long before the desert heat can despoil the setting, Daniel stands at Nebuchadnezzar's side, next to the seated king's throne, in the shade of the palace's outdoor pavilion. Thousands upon thousands of Babylonians and Jews are being herded out of the city and onto a broad desert plain. Daniel watches with regret as the chief priests and soldiers of Babylon assemble on the plain. The subject of all this exuberant commotion is a giant golden statue. It is ninety feet tall and nine feet wide.

Now Nebuchadnezzar raises his royal arm. This is the signal the trumpeters have been waiting for. A single note floats through the air. Instantly, the crowds grow silent and drop to their knees in worship of the statue and Nebuchadnezzar. Everyone bows: chief priests, soldiers, Jews, Babylonians. Everyone.

Daniel's worst fears are made manifest as his friends Hananiah, Mischael, and Azariah refuse to bow. They alone remain standing, refusing to honor any god but their own. "With all our heart, we follow you," Azariah prays aloud to the God of Abraham.

The trumpeters lower their horns. The desert plain is silent save for the screaming of the chief priests, who are demanding that the three faithful Jews fall to their knees.

"We fear and seek your presence," the prayer continues. This time the words come from the mouth of Mischael.

Now guards are wading into the crowd, eager to beat on the slaves. But the three of them remain standing. Daniel looks on from the distance. "Oh, my dear friends. Your faith will be tested now," he marvels to himself.

Even as Daniel speaks, the guards seize his friends. Daniel follows close behind as Nebuchadnezzar bolts from his throne and makes his way out from his shaded awning. The crowd parts instantly as the king strides toward the rebels. Daniel hurries alongside. Ahead of him, he sees his friends' hands being bound.

"They will serve you faithfully all their lives, as I will," Daniel reassures Nebuchadnezzar, searching for the soothing words that will calm the king. "But—"

"Your friends will bow—or I will make them bow," he replies.

But even when the guards try to force the three Israelites to their knees, they do not utter a word of worship to King Nebuchadnezzar. They seem fearless, which unleashes the king's legendary temper.

Daniel does not fear for his friends any longer, for he knows that God is near. He sees the silhouette of a fourth figure standing guard over Hananiah, Mischael, and Azariah. The fiery silhouette offers a blessing to the three men.

This is not an apparition that only Daniel can see. Nebuchadnezzar's face has grown white as he sees this mysterious presence. His chief priests are mumbling incantations, summoning their own gods to protect them. These men have claimed to be spiritual their whole lives, and yet this is the first time they've actually seen and felt the presence of God.

"The Lord hears my weeping. The Lord hears my cries for mercy. The Lord accepts my prayers," Daniel prays.

Hananiah, Mischael, and Azariah are completely unharmed. Tears in his eyes, Daniel gives a humble thanks to God.

As his chief priests turn and leave, desperate to escape any wrath that this God of Daniel's might want to inflict, Nebuchadnezzar sinks to his knees. He grasps Daniel's leg in an act of supplication and something else. Something for which Daniel has prayed for many, many years.

That something is faith. Nebuchadnezzar is deeply impressed by the power of God.

In the grandstand of Nebuchadnezzar's folly, God showed up. His power is there for the entire world to see. Guided by Daniel, Nebuchadnezzar soon allows the captive Jews to worship their God in peace.

Twenty-three years after Nebuchadnezzar's death, a new king gallops toward Babylon. He rides a splendid white horse and leads an army tens of thousands strong. This man is from the east, and he wears a heavy gold crown, lest anyone not know that he is king. For three years, this king of all Persia has swept across the land. He has conquered everything in his path, and now he rides forth to take control of Babylon. This is his greatest prize of all: his gateway to the west and the south, possessor of the plundered riches of Egypt and Israel.

High on a tower in the center of the city, Daniel stands among a group of royal ministers, watching the coming army. Among the group are his lifelong friends Hananiah, Mischael, and Azariah. They are all in their sixties now, and they have spent the vast majority of their lives in this foreign land. But they do not call it home. They never will. They don't fear the new king—they welcome him. To them, he is a liberator. Daniel has studied the new king and knows that the people in every territory that the Persian conquers have been left free to live and worship in their own traditions. Daniel smiles and says: "He will set us exiles free."

But when Daniel shares his visions from the God of Abraham with the Persian king, prayer is banned. In his kingdom, it will be a crime punishable by death. Daniel must pray in secret for weeks. One day, though, he is caught and thrown into the dungeon.

Daniel can endure the solitude of prison. Perhaps the king will change his mind. All things are possible with God. But he suddenly realizes he's not in a prison cell. He's in a lion's den.

Daniel stands completely still as one of the beasts stirs. The animal's body stretches at least eight feet long, and its massive paws are as big as Daniel's head. The lion sniffs the air. It rises and walks slowly toward

Daniel, the thick pads of those magnificent paws not making a single sound on the stone floor. Then it roars. A tear forms in the corner of Daniel's eye as the lion saunters toward him. Daniel falls to the ground and curls his body into a very small ball—the smallest he can possibly make. The damp floor of the cell feels calming against his cheek as he awaits the death that is soon to come. The other lions are awake now. Daniel doesn't know how many. Could be three. Could be six, for all he knows. They roar and grunt as they assemble. Daniel squeezes his eyes closed, knowing that there is absolutely no way to fight these beasts.

But then he remembers a way. "Lord, hear me. We do not make requests of you because we are righteous, but because of your great mercy," he prays to God. A sense of calm fills Daniel. He realizes God is providing this peace. So he continues: "Thank you, Lord. Thank you for my life and its many joys. Thank you for your love. And thank you, even now, for what is about to happen. For I know that it is your will, and that some greater good will come from my death."

He pulls himself into an even tighter ball. The lions now stand over him. The tears flow now, pooling on the floor. Daniel thinks of the people he loves and whom he will never see again. He thinks of the majesty of a sunrise, and the magnificence of the stars shining in the nighttime sky. All these wonders of life are about to be taken away.

"Your words are heard," says a voice.

Slowly, cautiously, Daniel raises his head. A tear slides from his cheek.

An angel stands before him. "You are innocent in the eyes of the Lord," the angel says.

That instant, all Daniel's fear vanishes. He uncurls himself from his tiny ball and rises to his feet. Daniel stands before the lions, completely unafraid. Whatever will happen, will happen. The lions are God's creations, no different from man. And God has dominion over all of his creations.

Daniel is ready for anything.

⎯⎯⎯⎯⎯◦⎯⎯⎯⎯⎯

Daniel and his God are haunting the Persian king's dreams. He wakes in a panic, seeing the truth for the first time, and he quickly gets out of bed. Throwing on a robe, he races through the palace toward the dungeon.

"Your God is real," he chants as he runs, "your God will save you. Your God is real, your God will save you." A long hallway finally leads to the stairwell down into the dungeon. "Open it!" the new king screams into the night. "Open it!"

The thick wooden door is flung open. The king steps inside. His guards draw swords and move to go with him, but he waves them away. One of them hands him a torch, which he accepts. The flames reveal a sleeping lion. They also reveal a sleeping Daniel, his head resting quite comfortably on the lion's chest.

The Persian gazes upon the sight in utter disbelief. Daniel is completely unharmed. The king swings his torch from lion to lion to lion—all are asleep.

Daniel stands. The king drops his torch and embraces him. Then the two men fall to their knees in prayer.

The years of exile are now at an end. The Persian decrees that the Jews may return to Jerusalem, taking the treasures looted from their temple, so that it might be rebuilt.

PART SIX

HOPE

Five hundred years pass. The Israelites have reestablished themselves in the Promised Land, free to practice their religion, but they are still oppressed. Herod, a king controlled by the Romans, rules over them.

In the small village of Nazareth, Mary, a young woman pure of heart, is walking home just like any other day. But today an angel of the Lord stands before her on the road. "Mary," he says softly, "I am Gabriel. Don't be afraid. The Lord is with you. You have found favor with God. Soon you will give birth to a child, and you are to call him Jesus. He will be great and will be known as the Son of the Most High."

"How can that be?" she asks.

"The Holy Spirit will come upon you. And the power of the Most High will overshadow you."

Mary's hands press against her stomach, as if she can already feel an energy there. "I am the Lord's servant.

May it be done to me as you have said," she says to Gabriel.

⟨∼⟩

Mary hides her pregnancy for as long as she can, not knowing how she can explain it to her husband-to-be, Joseph. Finally, the time comes. He notices.

"Tell me what's going on, Mary. Please."

"Joseph," she whispers. "There has been no one. I swear to you. This is God's work. An angel of the Lord appeared to me, telling me that I would be with child. He is to be the Messiah."

Joseph breaks away. He circles the room like an animal in a cage.

She reaches for his hands again. "My love, please believe me. I am telling you the truth."

"I want to believe," he says softly. "But God would not send the Messiah to people like us." Although he is a direct descendant of King David, Joseph is but a lowly carpenter. He opens the door, walks out, and doesn't look back. Only then does this mountain of a man let himself cry.

⟨∼⟩

Joseph wanders the streets of Nazareth alone. "God help me," Joseph prays. "Help me find a way to do the right thing." Joseph leans against a wall, lost in his thoughts. People stare at him. He doesn't care. Joseph's head droops and his shoulders sag. He closes his eyes in prayer and falls into a dream state.

"Joseph," a voice says. "Joseph." The angel Gabriel now stands powerfully before Joseph, the hood of his cloak pulled around his soft and tender face. His eyes seem to peer straight into Joseph's soul. Gabriel reaches for Joseph's hands. "Take Mary as your wife," commands Gabriel. "She is telling you the truth. She is pure. The child she carries is from God."

A stunned Joseph stares into the divine beauty of the angel. The weight upon his heart is gone. He wipes a tear of joy from his eye, and in that instant Gabriel is gone. Joseph emerges from his dream, elated, and races to Mary's home to tell her that he believes her. They are to name the baby Jesus.

One translation of the name is "God rescues." It also means "God saves." To many in Israel, the notion of a Messiah is a king like David, a savior who will deliver them from oppression. God, however, has something far bigger in mind. God will remain God, yet also become human in Jesus. He will save not just Israel but the entire world.

———∽———

Periodically the Romans demand a census. No matter where citizens are residing, they must return to the town of their ancestry to be counted. Now happily married, Joseph and Mary strap their belongings to a donkey and set off for the town of Bethlehem, the city where King David was born. The sun has not yet risen, and the morning air is cold.

They soon come upon a sight so utterly astonishing that Joseph's eyes widen. It is the most brilliant star he has ever seen, shining clear and low in the southern sky. Its brightness is a lamp unto their feet, and a light unto their path. Joseph squeezes Mary's hand. This is a sign God is with them.

———∽———

Herod sees the unusual star shining in the east but thinks nothing of it until the lavishly dressed Balthazar, a sage who has traveled by camel all the way from Persia, is escorted into the royal chamber. "So what brings you here, oh Prince?" Herod demands, his voice echoing off the marble pillars.

"The star. The new star rises in the east. I have followed its progress. The star is a sign that a great man is coming," Balthazar answers.

Herod glares at him. Not wanting to ignite Herod's legendary temper, Balthazar goes on to explain how the star guided him to Jerusalem.

But Herod isn't listening. He stares intently at Balthazar. "Every week," he finally says, "someone claims to be the chosen one. But those are mostly madmen in the marketplace—easily ignored, and just as easily silenced. So are you telling me that I should take your charts and your belief in a chosen one seriously?"

"Very seriously, sire." Balthazar once again motions for his men to step forward. This time they hold gifts in their arms. "We bring this chosen one presents fit for a king," he tells Herod.

That gets Herod's attention. "King?"

"Yes, Majesty. This man will become King of the Jews."

An awkward silence fills the chamber.

Herod's eyebrows rise. "Really?" he says through pursed lips.

"Yes, Majesty. This is from God. This is prophesied. The heavens testify to his arrival."

Herod smiles warmly, feigning a religiosity that he does not possess. "It has been testified? Really? If that is so, then we must do something immediately to pay homage."

Then Herod dismisses Balthazar with a wave of his hand, walks to a terrace, and gazes out over Jerusalem. There, in the midst of darkness and turmoil, rises the star.

Herod curses. "I am king of the Jews. And I will forever remain king of the Jews," he vows to himself. "I will keep my throne."

⁓

Mary groans. "It won't be long now, Joseph," she says.

"We're getting close to Bethlehem. I'll hurry," he replies, picking up the pace.

To their shock, the streets of Bethlehem are a sea of people, all of them looking for somewhere to sleep. They've all traveled there for the census. The young couple looks around, overwhelmed by the numbers.

"Thousand upon thousands," Joseph exclaims. "Why do they make us all register at once?" He pulls the donkey under an archway, where other people already huddle.

"I'll find a place," Joseph says. He leaves Mary and the donkey and then runs, searching for somewhere warm and private where she can deliver the baby.

But no such shelter exists in Bethlehem that night. Joseph is turned away time and time again. The inn-keepers are kind but insistent: there is no room.

A local takes pity on them. He directs Joseph to a small cave used as a barn—called a grotto—that smells of animals and grain. Sheep and cows clutter the small space. Joseph and Mary eagerly step inside.

<hr />

Joseph holds the tiny newborn baby up to the light. A smile of wonder crosses Joseph's face, for he has never known such joy. He brings the child to Mary. As she holds her son, the baby Jesus, her face transforms from tired and drained to radiantly joyful.

A crowd starts to gather. The star has led many to this site. The same angelic intervention that brought Mary and Joseph to Bethlehem has also spread the news to those who need to hear it most: locals, shep-herds, neighbors, and ordinary people. These are the ones whom Jesus has come to save, and for them to be standing in this small barn on this cold night is a moment unlike any other in time. They are witnessing the dawning of a new era—the fulfillment of the new covenant between God and humanity.

Between Herod's palace and Bethlehem, Prince Balthazar, atop an adorned camel, greets and falls into step with two Nubian wise men. They ride elegantly on their camels, ecstatic about the prospect of meeting this great new savior.

Suddenly the mass of farmworkers, children, and shepherds parts as royal attendants quietly and very efficiently clear a path. The crowd backs away, eyes lowered in deference.

Joseph is uneasy. The last thing he wants is trouble.

Balthazar steps forward. He has changed into his finest robes and wears a gold headdress. His behavior is not regal, however. "I am humbled," he murmurs as he drops to his knees. He has brought gifts for the newborn child. Balthazar looks to Mary and says to her, "Lady, I believe your son is the chosen king of his people. What is his name?"

Mary gently kisses her child on the forehead. "Jesus," she tells Balthazar, surprised to see that the Nubians have also come to see her child. "His name is Jesus."

These fine kings all bow down on the dirty ground before the newborn Jesus.

The crowd departs well into the night. The Magi do not return to tell Herod what they saw or where they found Jesus, because they learn in a dream that Herod has cruel intentions. They return to their homeland by a very different route.

Exhausted, Mary and Joseph are alone for the first time since Jesus' birth. The animals in their stalls are sound asleep, and the new parents soon fall into a deep slumber, too. The infant is swaddled and lying atop a feeding trough. The trough, which rests on a pile of hay, is called a manger. Joseph lies on the floor next to Mary, his muscles aching from the long days on the road. It feels good to get some rest, and even better to know that their son has entered the world safely. In the morning they can be counted for the census. Soon they can return home to Nazareth, where Joseph's carpentry business awaits.

Then one night, Joseph dreams of children being taken by Herod's soldiers. He must save Jesus. Joseph wakes up in a panic. His dream felt so real that he is actually stunned to behold Mary and Jesus sound asleep. But Joseph knows God speaks to prophets in many ways, including in dreams. He is sure God has given him the dream, and he knows what he must do next.

He must take his family and flee to Egypt.

By the time Herod's reign is over and it is safe to return to Nazareth, Jesus is five years old. Mary and Joseph know Jesus is destined by God to do something special. His knowledge of scripture can be a little startling at times, because it is so complex and thorough for his young age, but otherwise he behaves just like a normal boy. He does chores. He helps his father at work. He loves animals. He spends part of each day with Mary, his beloved mother, who carried the Son of God and knows his life will be extraordinary. Sometimes he's such a normal child that it's hard for Mary and Joseph to remind themselves that an angel once proclaimed to them that he is the promised King of the Jews.

God has sent someone to prepare the way, to start opening the hearts and minds of the people. He is strong in spirit, intensely driven, and pure of heart. His clothes are made from the hair of a camel, and he eats locusts and wild honey for food. This prophet shuns the corruption of the towns and cities for the purity of the wilderness. He lives as he preaches, in simple and uncompromising terms. What he demands from his growing legions of followers is that they change their lives, repent their sinful ways, and commit themselves to the Lord's path. His goal is nothing less than to light a new fire in the hearts and minds of thousands of Jews. The prophet's name is John. He is called John the Baptist because he baptizes followers of God by immersing them completely in the Jordan River, symbolically cleaning away their sins.

John baptizes people from miles around, helping them prepare their hearts for the coming of the Messiah, bringing them back to God, one baptism at a time. But many don't just come to be baptized. Many who step into the Jordan at John's behest believe that John himself is actually the Messiah.

"There is one to come, more powerful than I, whose sandals I am not fit to carry," John always tells those who ask. "*He* is the Messiah. Trust me, you'll know him when you see him."

But John sees him first. From out of the crowd steps

Jesus, now a young man and ready to leave his trade as a carpenter and begin his life's work.

The crowds along the shore notice the look in John's eyes. They turn to Jesus, wondering what makes him so special.

"Surely I need to be baptized by you," John says humbly. "And yet you come to me?"

Jesus gently takes hold of John's hand and places it atop his own head. "Let this be so now, John. It is proper for us to do this to fulfill all righteousness."

John nods in understanding. With all the people along the shore looking on, John the Baptist immerses Jesus in the cold waters of the Jordan. And in that moment, the weight of John's ministry becomes lighter. He is no longer a prophet, foreseeing the distant coming of the Messiah.

The Messiah is *here. Now.*

In the desert, Jesus must fight the greatest battle he has ever fought. He has traveled alone into the farthest reaches of this stark and waterless region. Before Jesus can take on the spiritual leadership of all humankind, he must confront and overcome his opponent—Satan.

Jesus staggers as he walks, on the verge of collapse

from hunger. The hem of his filthy robe drags along the ground. His face is swollen, and thirst is driving him mad. It has been forty days and nights since Jesus entered the desert—his personal wilderness. Forty days, one day for each of the forty years that Moses and the Israelites wandered in their own wilderness, seeking the Promised Land.

A snake slithers past, its tongue flicking at the dry desert air. Jesus recoils. The serpent is thick and powerful, poised to coil and strike in an instant. Jesus bends down carefully and selects a large rock. He grasps it firmly in his fist. He stands, and as he does, a shadow appears.

"If you are the Son of God," Satan speaks from the shadow, "tell the stones to become bread."

"Man shall not live by bread alone," Jesus calmly informs Satan, "but on every word that comes from the mouth of God."

Satan turns away in disgust and simply vanishes.

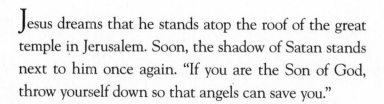

Jesus dreams that he stands atop the roof of the great temple in Jerusalem. Soon, the shadow of Satan stands next to him once again. "If you are the Son of God, throw yourself down so that angels can save you."

"Do not put the Lord your God to the test," Jesus warns Satan.

Jesus turns away from the edge. He dislodges a roof tile, which plummets to the cobbled courtyard below and shatters into a hundred pieces.

Now he awakes from the dream to find himself standing atop a mountain cliff. The desert stretches out far below him, as vast and wide as the eye can see, seemingly stretching to infinity. The shadow is next to him. "I will give you the whole world," promises Satan, "if you will bow down and worship me." The shadow extends his hand for Jesus to kneel down and kiss.

Jesus pushes it away. "Get away from me, Satan. It is written, 'Worship the Lord your God and serve him only.'" The Spirit of the Lord has come upon Jesus. He defiantly turns his back on Satan.

Rugged, upright, and sure, he walks out of the desert in the power of the Spirit to begin his mission. A single venomous snake slithers back into a hole in the ground.

Three fishermen finish a long night of trying to fill their nets. They have nothing to show for it. As they guide their boats onto the sandy beach, a distant figure can be seen walking their way. Peter notices him first.

"Who's that?" he says in a gruff tone.

"John says he is the Messiah," his brother Andrew responds.

"Oh, really? Can he teach you to find fish?"

"Yes, I can," Jesus replies.

Before Peter can stop him, Jesus walks over to his boat, takes hold of the hull, and shoves it back out into the water.

"Hey!" Peter barks. "What do you think you're doing? That's my boat. And you're not allowed to launch it all by yourself."

"You'd better help me, then," Jesus calmly replies.

Peter runs into the water and grabs the hull. But Jesus won't be stopped. He looks Peter in the eye and keeps pushing the boat out into the Sea of Galilee. Something in Peter's gut tells him to do as Jesus orders. He stops trying to pull the boat back toward shore and starts shoving it out to sea. When the water is waist deep, he pulls himself up into the boat. Jesus climbs aboard, too.

"What are we doing here?" Peter asks.

"Fishing."

Peter stares into those eyes one more time. "There are no fish out here."

"Peter," says Jesus, "I can show you where to find fish. What have you got to lose?"

Peter reaches for his nets, preparing to cast.

Jesus shakes his head. "Go farther," he commands.

Peter looks at him. "You've never fished here. So listen when I tell you—there are no fish out there at this time of day."

"Please."

So Peter guides his boat into deeper waters.

"Blessed are they who hunger after righteousness," Jesus says. "For they shall be filled."

"Who are you?" Peter demands. "Why are you here?"

"Ask and it will be given to you; look and you will find."

What follows is a day of fishing unlike any other in Peter's life. Thousands of fish fill his nets. His shoulders burn from the strain of pulling them all into the boat. His nets begin to tear. But Peter casts again and again and again, and every time the nets come back full. Other boats soon set out from the shore as Peter is forced to call for help.

As the day ends, Peter collapses atop the pile of fish filling the hold. "How did this happen?" he asks Jesus. He can feel a tear welling in his eye. Something tells him that the direction of his life has just changed.

Jesus does not respond.

"Teacher, I am a sinner," Peter tells Jesus. "I am not a seeker, just a mere fisherman."

"So follow me," Jesus finally says. "And don't be afraid. Follow me and I will make you a fisher of men."

PART SEVEN

MISSION

A foreign army still controls the country. People suffer from taxes and the excesses of the Roman rulers. Some days their bodies and spirits are sapped of energy, and they can't remember a time when they weren't drained and beaten down. This simple marketplace of friends and neighbors, and food for sustenance, offers a few moments of peace.

For one woman in the crowd, there is no peace. Her mind has snapped, and she is tormented by inner voices. Her face is dirty and contorted from her suffering, and she sweats profusely.

When Peter reaches out to help her, she spits in his face and lunges into the mass of people.

"Leave her!" someone yells to him. "She's possessed by demons. You can't help her."

Peter doesn't give up. He presses through the crowd, right behind the woman. She breaks through into an open space, grabs a pot from a stall, and then hurls it at Peter. She turns to run once again, but finds herself standing face-to-face with Jesus. "What do you want?" she bawls at him, completely unafraid. Her eyes are clouded with confusion and rage.

When Jesus says nothing, she marches right up to him, raises the broken pot above her head, and stares into his eyes.

"Come out of her!" Jesus commands the demons.

Violent energy whooshes out of the woman. Her face freezes in shock, and she collapses. She sobs and shakes as the demons leave her, one by one. Finally, she looks up into Jesus' eyes once again and finds herself transformed.

Jesus gently places his hand on her forehead. "I will strengthen you and help you," he tells her.

She smiles. Her mind is clear, as if she has just emerged from a nightmare.

"What is your name?" Jesus asks.

"Mary. Mary of Magdala."

"Come with me, Mary."

Peter watches Jesus approach him. The fisherman shakes his head in wonder. He knows that she has just learned what Peter and the other men who have joined Jesus already know: he embodies God's promise of salvation.

Peter studies the faces of others in the crowd. They express wonder at the instant change that has come over the madwoman Mary. He hears their whispers: "It's him...." "It's that preacher...." "It's the prophet...."

Others are cynical. They've seen it all before. They're suspicious of this quiet carpenter.

The Roman soldiers study Jesus as if he is a threat.

But Jesus' every action is one of peace. "Love one another," he tells his followers. "By this will all men know that you are my disciples, if you love one another."

The sound of coins being dropped onto the counting tables fills the air. Jesus and his disciples now pass by the lines of sullen men who wait to pay their taxes.

Jesus is carefully watching one of the tax collectors. The man's name, the disciples are soon to learn, is Levi. Despite appearing soft or even supportive to his fellow Jews, he is a tax collector nonetheless.

"What do you see, Lord?" asks the disciple named John—not John the Baptist, who is now imprisoned.

Jesus doesn't answer. His gaze has been so hard and so direct that soon Levi raises his head to stare back at this powerful energy he feels. His eyes connect with those of Jesus, just as the Son of God issues the following order: "Follow me." Levi stands up and walks away from the table, leaving piles of uncounted coins in his wake. From now on, he will be called Matthew.

The disciples are furious.

"You don't like that I talk to tax collectors and sinners," Jesus says. "But search your heart and hear what I have to say: it's not the healthy who need a doctor, but the sick. I'm not here to call the righteous. I'm here for the sinners."

Jesus squats in the town square, drawing in the dust with his finger. He is drawing not a picture but a series of letters. He is not alone, nor is the scene tranquil. Directly behind him, a crowd is gathering. A woman is forced to stand in front of a high wall, facing this crowd. Between the woman and the crowd rises a pile of smooth, large stones. When the time comes, each man in the group will be asked to lift a stone from a pile and throw it at her. The young woman standing before the wall has been accused of adultery. She is an outcast in the local society. The men in the crowd grasp their stones, eager to throw.

Jesus, meanwhile, scribbles in the dirt.

The disciples cry out to Jesus: "Please, say something to help her."

Then, to the shock of all who watch, Jesus reaches down and selects a fine throwing stone from the pile. Jesus walks over and lines up next to the high priests, or Pharisees, each of whom now holds a stone, facing the condemned woman.

Now the crowd sees the words Jesus has written: JUDGE NOT, LEST YOU BE JUDGED.

As they stare at the words, letting them rest upon their hearts, Jesus strolls back and forth in front of the throwing line. He holds his rock up in his hand for all to see as he scrutinizes the rocks held by the others. "Let the man who is without sin throw the first stone." Jesus offers his rock to each man, with the utter certainty that they all have sinned.

Even the Pharisees cannot look Jesus in the eye.

Jesus walks over to the woman. Behind, he hears the dull thuds of rocks hitting the earth. But the rocks are being dropped, not thrown. Each man turns silently and walks quickly home as his own sins weigh on his conscience.

"Go," Jesus tells the woman. "Go and sin no more."

It's dusk as Jesus and his disciples walk up a long hill that leads to the next town. Children run to greet them, but otherwise it appears that they are in for an ordinary evening. They'll find a place to sleep and get a meal. Perhaps Jesus will teach, or maybe he won't. All in all, they're just glad to be sleeping with a roof over their heads after many a night sleeping outdoors.

But as Jesus leads the way up and over the top of the hill, the apostles gasp in shock. Thousands upon thousands of people fill the valley below. They stand on the shores of a silvery sea, waiting anxiously to hear the words of Jesus.

The instant the crowds catch sight of him, they rush up the hillside, all trying to get a spot in front when Jesus begins teaching.

"Would you look at all those people!" gasps Peter.

"Yes," Jesus answers. "How are we going to feed them all?"

"Do what?"

"Feed them. It's late. I don't see any cooking fires. They must be famished. Go out into the crowd," Jesus tells his disciples. "And bring back as much food as you can."

They come back with almost nothing: five loaves of bread and two fish. There's not enough to feed the disciples themselves, let alone roughly five thousand.

The crowd consumed the contents of their food baskets hours ago as they waited patiently for Jesus. Now those baskets are quite empty.

Jesus seems unbothered. "Thank you, Father," he prays over the little food they have gathered. "Thank you for what you bring us."

The disciples begin to distribute the food, and the baskets overflow with bread and fish—so much that the crowd has seconds, and then thirds.

The crowd is soon demanding more food and clamoring to proclaim Jesus as the new King of the Jews. But he sends them away, knowing that the miracle they observed will be more than enough to fortify their faith for some time to come.

Jesus has restored sight to the blind, cured the lame, cast out demons, and healed the handicapped. Some say that if a person has enough faith in Jesus and his teachings, the sick can be healed, the physical body can be made whole, and life itself can be restored.

Jesus is soon put to the test as he and his disciples walk through a village, enjoying the games played by the young children and the generally festive atmosphere of the day. A messenger comes running with a desperate plea. He tells Jesus that his friend Lazarus lies dangerously ill.

Jesus and his disciples make the walk to Lazarus's village, and they find a town consumed in grief.

"I am the resurrection and the life," Jesus tells Lazarus's sisters, Martha and Mary. "If anyone believes in me, he will live, even though he dies. And whoever lives and believes in me will never die. Do you believe this?"

"Yes, Lord. I believe that you are the Christ, the Son of God who was to come into the world." Mary weeps as she speaks, and Jesus is deeply moved.

"Where have you laid him?" Jesus asks. By now Lazarus has been dead for four days.

They lead him to their brother's tomb to grieve. Jesus weeps.

"Take away the stone," Jesus commands.

The disciples and the men of the village obey Jesus' order and roll back the stone that covers the entrance to the tomb. Word has spread throughout the village that Jesus is at the tomb, and now hundreds have gathered, curious.

"Lazarus," Jesus shouts boldly. "Come out!"

Lazarus's sisters sob, worn out from false hope, then days of mourning. Then a uniform gasp erupts from the crowd and many fall on their faces in worship as they stare at Lazarus, wrapped in his burial garments. His head is uncovered, and he squints as he steps into the sunlight. He is alive.

Jesus speaks again, but in a voice so loud and authoritative that it can be heard a hundred yards away. "Whoever believes in me shall never die. *Never!*"

Martha collapses in shock. Her sister, Mary, is shaking. John laughs, incredulous. Tears run down Peter's cheeks. "It's true," he tells Jesus. "You really are the Messiah."

PART EIGHT

BETRAYAL

It is the week before Passover, that holy day that marks the time in Jewish history when its people were spared from death and led out of slavery from Egypt. Right now, even as all of Israel prepares to celebrate this most important and sacred occasion, one very select group of pilgrims is making its way to Jerusalem.

The people of the city have heard about Jesus for years, and they now celebrate his arrival. Hundreds of people line his path, throwing palm branches onto the ground to carpet the road. They chant "hosanna," which means "save us," for even more than a spiritual teacher, these people hope that Jesus is the new King of the Jews. They believe he has come to save them from the Romans. "Hosanna," they chant. "Hosanna, hosanna, hosanna, hosanna." The roar is deafening, and Jesus acknowledges them all with a smile and a wave. The disciples walk on either side of him, somewhat dazzled by the excitement.

"Look at all the people," marvels Mary Magdalene.

"I never, in my wildest dreams, thought we would ever see something like this," John agrees.

Thomas can't believe what he's seeing, and even Peter, that most practical of all men, is dazzled. "This," he gasps, "is incredible."

Jesus has chosen to make his entry into Jerusalem on a donkey because scripture foretells that the King of the Jews will enter Jerusalem as a humble man riding on a donkey. The symbolism is not lost on the crowd, who know their scripture well.

"It is written!" they cry in the midst of their hosannas, clapping and chanting and waving palm fronds as a sign of faithfulness. Their faces are alight with hope. This is the One, the man who will bring a new peaceful age, free from poverty and suffering.

A donkey?" Caiaphas, leader of the Sanhedrin, fumes when a servant tells him of Jesus' mode of transportation.

The elders of the temple stand with him, shaking their heads. Jesus' arrival represents a direct challenge to the Jewish authorities. Claims that Jesus is the Messiah have outraged them. Only they can anoint the new Messiah, and this carpenter from Nazareth is clearly not such a man.

"See, your king comes to you," Caiaphas sarcastically quotes from scripture. "Triumphant and victorious, humble and riding on a donkey."

The elders say nothing.

"And where is he headed?" Caiaphas asks the servant.

The servant lowers his head. What he's about to say next will not be the words that Caiaphas or the elders want to hear.

"The temple," he says.

"The temple!"

One of the elders, a man named Nicodemus, quotes another verse: "To lead his people to victory and throw out the oppressors."

"The crowds," Caiaphas demands of the servant. "How are they responding?"

The servant's name is Malchus. He had hoped to impress the Sanhedrin by racing to tell them Jesus' whereabouts. Yet it seems that every word that comes from his mouth is just another variation of bad news. So he says nothing.

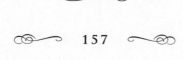

Jesus reaches the outer court of the great Jerusalem temple complex—the Court of the Gentiles, as it is known. The disciples stay close as Jesus stops walking and studies all that is going on around him. His face and eyes are the picture of sadness. He sees more than just animals and money changers: an old man being shooed away by an angry money changer, a poor family trying to buy a lamb but having only enough for doves, a frail old woman being jostled, and a lost little girl crying. The commotion makes it impossible for anyone to engage in devout prayer. Jesus' face clouds with anger and resentment. He walks calmly toward the stall where the money changers have set up shop. Coins are piled on the tables. Their hands are dirty from counting money. They banter with one another. Jesus grabs the table edge with two hands and flips it over. Then he goes on to the next table and does the same. All heads in the temple court turn to the sound of spilling coins, and onlookers immediately race to scoop up the fallen money. "What are you doing?" shrieks one money changer.

But Jesus is not done. He cannot be stopped. On to the next table.

Jesus flips another table, which bounces against a birdcage and sets loose a flock of doves.

"Why?" asks one vendor, disconsolate about all his

earnings now scattered on the temple floor. "Why have you done this?"

"Is it not written?"

"What on earth could you possibly mean?"

"Is it not written?" Jesus repeats, but this time in a booming voice that echoes throughout the chamber. In an instant, the entire court is silent.

"My house...my house shall be called a house of prayer," Jesus continues. "But you have turned it into a den of thieves."

Peter and John hold back the angry merchants as they attempt to punish Jesus, who has finished this task and is marching out of the court. In his wake are tipped tables, angry traders, and a scene of total chaos.

Nicodemus from the Sanhedrin steps forward.

"Who are you to tell us this? How dare you? It is *we* who interpret God's law—not you."

"You're more like snakes than teachers of the law," Jesus replies in a heated tone.

Nicodemus is beyond shocked. "Wait. You can't say that! We uphold the law. We serve God."

"No," Jesus replies. "You pray lofty prayers. You strut about the temple, impressed by your own piety. But you are just hypocrites."

Nicodemus is stunned. Men of his rank are simply not spoken to in this manner.

Jesus reaches out and gently lifts the fine material of Nicodemus's robe, rubbing the delicate threads between his fingers. "It is much harder for a rich person to enter the Kingdom of God than it is for a camel to go through the eye of a needle," Jesus tells him, letting go of the robe.

Everyone in the temple has heard Jesus' words. The Jewish pilgrims who have traveled so far to be there for Passover are inspired by such a courageous stance against the rich and powerful men of the religious establishment, who have oppressed their own people as much as the Romans have. Only they've used threats and God's law instead of brute force to control the people.

Nicodemus looks about uneasily. He feels trapped. The crowd is definitely on Jesus' side. At the far end of the chamber, he sees the Roman soldiers prepared to move in if the situation gets out of hand.

As Jesus leaves the temple, he is followed by the disciples, a crowd of excited new followers, and a few Jewish elders who want to know more about Jesus' teachings. Malchus trails far behind, working as Caiaphas's spy.

Jesus leads this unlikely procession of old friends,

new friends, elders, and a spy down the temple steps, then suddenly stops, turns, and faces them.

Malchus does his best to appear as if he's there accidentally, but his purpose is now clear.

Jesus ignores him. Instead, despite the huge crowd, he speaks to his disciples as if no one else is there. "Do you see this great building?" he tells them. "I tell you that not one stone of this place will be left standing."

Peter and John look at each other. Did Jesus really say what they thought he said? Is he really threatening to destroy the temple?

A Jewish elder has heard Jesus' words, and questions him. "Who are you to say these things?"

Jesus continues talking to his disciples: "Destroy this temple and I will build it again in three days."

"How is this possible?" the elder asks.

Jesus doesn't answer him. He abruptly turns and continues on his way, leaving his disciples scratching their heads about what Jesus means by his comments.

Caiaphas and the high priests are gathered, discussing the situation with Nicodemus, his servant Malchus, and his handpicked group of elders.

"He said what?" asks an incredulous Caiaphas.

Malchus is the first to reply: "That he would destroy the temple."

"I am shocked. He claims to be a man of God, and then says he plans to destroy the house of our Lord?"

Caiaphas remains silent, steadying himself against the shock waves pounding his body. This is far worse than he thought. Finally, he speaks. "We must act fast. Very fast. But with care. We cannot arrest him openly. His supporters will riot, and then Rome will crack down." Caiaphas pauses, thinking through a new plan. "We must arrest him quietly at night. Before Passover. What was the name of that friend of his?"

"Judas," Malchus answers.

"Yes, Judas. Bring him here. Discreetly."

Malchus nods and makes a hasty exit.

The following evening Jesus and his disciples pray together, asking that God bless their meal and their fellowship. The unleavened bread in front of them is hot from the oven, and its fresh-baked smell fills the room. After the prayer, the disciples relax, reclining on cushions. But before they can eat, Jesus stuns them with devastating news. This is their last meal together.

Jesus tears off a piece of bread. "This is my body," he tells them all. "Take of it and eat."

John has tears streaming down his cheeks, but he understands. He opens his mouth, and Jesus places a morsel of the bread on his tongue.

Then Jesus raises a cup of wine. "This is my blood. I will shed my blood so that your sins may be forgiven."

Bread and wine pass from hand to hand around the room. "Remember me by doing this. Soon I will go to be with the Father, but when you eat my bread and drink from my cup, you proclaim my glory, and I am with you always.

"But now I must tell you," Jesus says, as the disciples pay close attention, "one of you here in this room will betray me."

The wine is passed to Judas. He struggles to keep his composure, his eyes now riveted on Jesus.

"Who is it?" asks John. "Which one of us would do such a thing?"

Jesus tears off a piece of bread and passes it. "Whoever eats this will betray me."

All the disciples stare, transfixed, as the piece of bread is passed to Judas. "It's not I," Judas protests, holding the bread in his hand but not eating. "Surely, I would never betray you, Lord."

Jesus' eyes stay fixed on Judas. Looking straight back at him, Judas takes the bread. He eats it and shudders.

The disciples are all staring at him with a look of pure horror.

"Do it quickly," Jesus commands Judas.

Terrified, Judas scrambles to his feet and makes for the door. A disgusted Peter chases after him, not sure whether he will beat Judas to within an inch of his life or merely follow to make sure that Judas does not carry out this betrayal.

But Jesus calls Peter back. "Peter, leave him. You will all fall away. Even you, Peter."

"Never, Lord. I am loyal. I would never betray you."

"Peter," Jesus tells him, "before the cock crows at dawn, you will have denied knowing me three times."

Before Peter can protest, Jesus rises to his feet. "Come. Let us all leave."

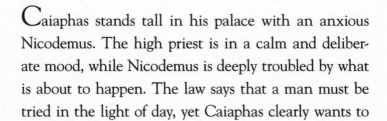

Caiaphas stands tall in his palace with an anxious Nicodemus. The high priest is in a calm and deliberate mood, while Nicodemus is deeply troubled by what is about to happen. The law says that a man must be tried in the light of day, yet Caiaphas clearly wants to condemn Jesus this very night.

"Judas is bringing him to us before dawn," says Caiaphas.

"But the law does not allow it," insists Nicodemus. "A trial must be held in daylight!"

"And does our law allow riots? Does our law invite Romans to spill Jewish blood? You were there. You heard what Pontius Pilate said."

Judas bursts into the room.

"Where is he?" Caiaphas asks.

"I don't know." Caiaphas fixes a stare on Judas, who admits, "But I do know where he is going."

Caiaphas points to Malchus. "Lead my servant to him."

The garden of Gethsemane is deserted except for Jesus and his disciples. He has spent the last hour in fervent prayer, but the disciples are curled up on the ground, fast asleep.

"The spirit is willing, but the body is weak. Wake up," Jesus demands after observing them for a moment. He needs them to bear witness. "Stay awake. The hour is at hand."

Jesus leaves them, walking slowly back up the hill, once again to be alone with his Father. He knows that

Judas is almost here, leading a group of men who will arrest him by force. To endure what is about to take place, Jesus needs strength. As he arrives atop the hill, he immediately falls to his knees in prayer, presses his forehead into the dusty ground, clasps his hands together, and prays: "Father, if you are willing, take this cup from me. Yet not my will, but yours be done." He is beset by confusion because he is both human and divine. He is racked with human fear of the great pain he will soon experience.

Jesus hears the sound of an approaching mob. Their torches light the base of the hill, and their excited voices cut through the night. Jesus' head is still bowed as he now prays for the strength to carry out God's plan. Sweat continues to fall. Now that God's will is confirmed, resolve washes over him. Not peace, for what he is about to endure cannot bring the gentle calm of peace. Just resolve. "Your will, Father, is mine."

Jesus rises from his knees and stands alone in the grove of olive trees. His disciples suddenly burst over the rise and surround him protectively. A line of torches looms in the darkness, marching steadily toward Jesus.

"The time has come," Jesus says to everyone and no one.

Judas has reappeared and kneels behind Jesus, as

if in prayer. Then he leans in and kisses Jesus on the cheek.

Jesus does not feel anger or contempt. He tells Judas, "Judas, you betray the Son of man with a kiss?" Jesus understands Judas's role is necessary for God's plan to be fulfilled.

A horrified Peter watches as Jesus is shoved forward, grasped on both arms by strong men and surrounded by a half-dozen others, hooded, and dragged off.

PART NINE

Deliverance

Jesus' followers have gathered at the temple. Disciples Mary and John make their way through the crowd of tents and sleeping, uneducated, largely unsophisticated pilgrims. The temple guards glare at them, recognizing them from their many appearances with Jesus.

Mary Magdalene notices the distraught face of Mary, the mother of Jesus. She wanders through the crowd. They rush to her side.

"Mary! John! Where is my son?"

"Jesus has been arrested, but we don't know where they've taken him," responds Mary Magdalene.

"Arrested?" replies Mary. "At night?" Ever since the angel Gabriel told her she was going to give birth to the Messiah, Mary has known this day would come.

John glances around at the crowds. "He's not here.

They must have taken him someplace secret. So they won't have any protests."

The sun rises low and red over the temple.

~~~

The doors of Caiaphas's palace swing open. Peter is standing just outside as Jesus is dragged out. Throughout the night, Peter's own life has been in jeopardy as he has waited to hear what has happened to Jesus, hoping somehow he can help.

Malchus reads from a proclamation: "Let it be known that Jesus of Nazareth has been tried by the supreme court of temple elders. He has been found guilty of blasphemy and threatening to destroy the temple. The sentence is death."

A large guard approaches Peter. "You…I know you."

Peter doesn't scare easily. "I don't know what you're talking about."

"You know him," says the guard, grabbing at Peter. "I heard you call him Rabbi."

"No," says Peter. "He's nothing to do with me."

"He's one of them," a woman screams, pointing at Peter.

He spins around and confronts her. "I tell you, I don't know him."

Peter sees Jesus being hauled away, and he is

frustrated by his inability to help Jesus, who means so much to him. The rooster crows, and Peter remembers Jesus' words that he would deny knowing his beloved friend and teacher before dawn. The rough, gruff man sobs in agony.

Pontius Pilate is tending to governmental matters when Caiaphas is announced.

"Governor, we need your help," says Caiaphas. "We have convicted a dangerous criminal and sentenced him to death."

"And? When is his execution?"

Caiaphas moves closer, spreading his hands as if in explanation. "We—the Sanhedrin—cannot carry it out. It's Passover, you see. It's against our law." Caiaphas punctuates his tale by bowing his head deferentially. Pilate looks at him with distaste.

"So do it after Passover," says Pilate. "Surely the man can live a few more days."

"Normally, I would say yes. But this man is an urgent threat—not only to us but also to Rome. He claims to be our king and is using that lie to whip my people into rebellion. This man could very well tear Jerusalem apart."

"I am quick to punish criminals," Pilate snarls, "but only if they break the law. I need proof that this man has done so—or Rome will not be pleased."

"He has broken the law, Prefect. I assure you," Caiaphas replies.

"You had better be right," Pilate grumbles, fixing Caiaphas with a deadly gaze. "If you're wasting my time, you'll pay for this." He looks at his guards. "I'll see the prisoner."

Jesus is held by two guards in Pilate's cells. Pilate looks at Jesus. After a long pause, he asks, "Are you the King of the Jews?"

Jesus says nothing.

"They say you claim to be King of the Jews."

"Is that what you think, or did others tell you this about me?" Jesus replies calmly, for he fears no man. Pilate takes a step back and momentarily averts his eyes.

"Your own people say that," Pilate replies, regaining his composure. "So tell me: are you a king?"

"My kingdom is not of this world," answers Jesus. "If it was, my servants would fight my arrest."

"So you are a king?"

"You say rightly that I am a king. I was born to come into the world and testify to the truth; everyone who is of truth hears my voice."

"Truth? What is truth?" demands Pilate.

Jesus says nothing. He smiles and looks up into the single shaft of light that penetrates the dark cell. It bathes his face.

Pilate greets Caiaphas and the elders with thinly veiled contempt. "I have met your Jesus and have come to the conclusion that he is guilty of nothing more than being deranged. That is not a crime in Rome."

"He's broken the law," Caiaphas protests.

"*Your* law," Pilate replies smoothly. "Not Caesar's." The Roman stares hard at Caiaphas. "Teach this man some respect. Give him forty lashes and dump him outside the city walls. That is my decree."

"Nothing more? I cannot be held responsible for what the people will do if you release a man who has broken our sacred laws. Especially on this day, when our eyes are on God."

"The people?" Pilate responds sarcastically. "Caesar decrees that I can release a prisoner at Passover. I shall let 'the people' decide which of the prisoners in my jails shall be crucified, and which shall be set free."

Jesus is dragged into the courtyard by two Roman soldiers. His face is crusted in blood, and his eyes are now swollen shut by a fresh round of beatings.

Mary, his mother, gasps. She stands outside in the crowd, peering into the courtyard through the grate.

The soldiers now retrieve their whips.

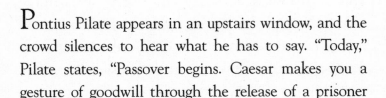

Pontius Pilate appears in an upstairs window, and the crowd silences to hear what he has to say. "Today," Pilate states, "Passover begins. Caesar makes you a gesture of goodwill through the release of a prisoner chosen by you.

"I give you a choice," Pilate tells them. "You may choose Barabbas, a murderer, or you may choose this other man—a teacher who claims to be your king."

Laughter and jeers spew forth from the crowd. Caiaphas, who now stands at Pilate's side, yells, "We have no king but Caesar."

Temple guards move through the crowd, whispering instructions and receiving nods of agreement. "Crucify him!" is spontaneously shouted by members of the crowd who have remained silent until now.

Mary, mother of Jesus, is horrified. Her hands go to her face, and she covers her mouth in dismay.

Pilate sees the look on Caiaphas's face and knows that he has an answer.

"Decide!" Pilate shouts to the crowd.

"Barabbas," they roar back. "Free Barabbas."

Pilate is mystified. He looks at Caiaphas and then back at the crowd. "You choose a murderer," he tells them with a shake of his head, then holds up a hand to silence the mob.

"Do it," he says to his guards. The bewildered soldiers reluctantly unlock Barabbas's shackles. The crowd cheers.

"And this wretch," Pilate yells to the crowd. "What shall I do with him?"

"Crucify him! Crucify him!"

Pilate silences the crowd. "How can you condemn this man and spare a murderer?"

"Crucify! Crucify! Crucify!"

"Very well," he tells them. "Crucify him."

Pilate reaches for a nearby bowl of water and washes his hands.

"I am innocent of this man's blood," he says.

Pilate dries his hands. This crucifixion is no longer his affair.

It has been just five days since Jesus was welcomed into Jerusalem. Now he is to be crucified on a hill outside the city walls, for Jewish law does not allow executions inside the city. Two criminals will also be crucified at the same time.

Jesus is in agony as he carries the cross to his crucifixion. His body is bent by the weight of the wood, and the crown of thorns inflicts a new burst of pain whenever the cross bumps against it. The many beatings he has endured in the hours since his capture make it hard to breathe.

Yet he sees everything. Both the sympathetic and not-so-sympathetic faces in the crowd. He also sees Mary, his mother. Jesus stumbles and feels the lash of a Roman whip as he falls. He reaches out to steady himself, pressing his hand flat against a stone wall.

The distance from Pilate's palace to Golgotha, the place where Jesus will die, is five hundred yards. Jesus knows he cannot make it. He drops the cross and crumples to the ground. Mary races forward to save her son, but a Roman guard grabs her roughly and throws her back.

"Please," John says, risking his life by stepping from the crowd. "She's his mother!"

Tears stream down Mary's cheeks. The Roman guard steps toward John with a menacing glare on his face, but the disciple is undeterred. "Have mercy. Please!"

Mary can't help herself. She flings herself forward and falls onto her knees, next to her son. She wraps her arms lovingly around him in what will surely be their last embrace. Jesus' eyes are swollen shut, and he can hardly react.

"My son," Mary sobs.

Jesus forces his eyes open. "Don't be afraid," he tells his mother. "The Lord is with you." His words repeat exactly what Gabriel told her when he visited her as a young virgin. They give her strength, and his look of love fills her with courage. She tries to help him up with the cross. If she could, she would carry it for him, but she knows this is what he came to do.

It is clear Jesus cannot carry the cross any farther. A man, Simon of Cyrene, is forced to shoulder the cross for Jesus. Their eyes lock, and then their hands link to lift the heavy wood. Together, they share the burden.

The crowd thins as Jesus leaves the city walls behind. Mary, John, and Mary Magdalene walk to the side of the road as it curls steeply upward. They are just out of Jesus' sight but always there. The hill is known as Golgotha, or "Place of the Skulls," because it is believed that the skull of Adam is buried there.

Choking dust fills the air, and Jesus can barely breathe. He trips. He rises and then trips again.

"My Lord," cries a woman as she steps into the street. Despite the threat of punishment by the guards, she lovingly washes his face with a cloth.

Jesus and Simon of Cyrene finally arrive at the place of crucifixion. Simon drops the heavy cross and quickly leaves. Jesus, no longer able to stand, collapses into the dust. The Roman guards spring into action.

The cross is upright. Jesus hangs from it. The executioner's job is done.

Meanwhile, those who have watched the crucifixion step forward. Mother Mary weeps with unbearable grief.

"Come to save others, can't even save yourself," mocks a Pharisee.

Jesus hears it all. He moans and then speaks to God: "Father, forgive them, for they know not what they do."

Black storm clouds now fill the sky as he knows that the time has come to leave this world.

"It is finished," Jesus says aloud. "Father, into your hands, I commend my spirit."

～～～

The body of Jesus, immaculately wrapped in linen, lies alone on a rock. Strong men roll the rock over the opening of the tomb to make sure that the body won't be disturbed. Night has fallen, so the burial party lights torches to guide the way back down the path.

The morning of the third day after Jesus' death, Mary Magdalene takes it upon herself to go visit the tomb. She misses Jesus enormously, and even the prospect of sitting outside his burial site is a source of comfort. Her eyes are tired as she ascends a small hill. She knows that even in the early-morning fog, she will be able to see the tomb from the top, and she begins looking once she gets there. The entrance to the tomb stands open. The rock has been moved aside. Mary begins to cry.

Where is Jesus?

PART TEN

NEW WORLD

Mary Magdalene hears a man's voice at the tomb's opening. "Why are you crying? Who are you looking for?"

It is the calm and knowing voice she recognizes well. Mary's heart soars as she realizes who is talking to her. "Jesus!" Her eyes swim with tears of joy and amazement as she steps out into the sunlight.

"Go and tell our brothers I am here."

Mary stares at Jesus in awe. Then he is gone. Mary, overcome with joy, sprints back into Jerusalem to tell the disciples the good news.

They stare in shock and disbelief at the empty tomb. Peering sheepishly inside from a few feet back, they can't see footprints or any other sign that tomb robbers have been there, but they know that's the obvious answer.

"Thieves," says Peter.

"That's right: tomb robbers," adds John.

Peter steps closer to the opening. A white circle of light suddenly shines inside. Peter moves toward the light and sees the unmistakable Jesus. "My Lord," he says, in a hushed voice. Peter reaches forth to touch Jesus. And then Jesus disappears.

A stunned Peter steps back out of the tomb. Mary sees the look on his face. "Now do you believe me?" she asks.

Peter hands John a strip of linen from the tomb. "But he's gone," John says, mystified.

"No, my brother," Peter assures him, that old confidence suddenly returned. "He is not gone. He's back!" An exuberant Peter takes off and races down the hill. On the way, he purchases a loaf of bread from a vendor.

"What happened?" asks Matthew as Peter, John, and Mary enter the building where the disciples have hidden since Jesus' crucifixion.

"A cup," Peter answers. "I need a cup."

Peter gives a piece of unleavened bread to John, who puts it slowly into his mouth. "His body," Peter reminds him. A cup is found and thrust into John's hand. Peter fills it with wine. "And his blood," Peter says.

Peter, suddenly transformed into the rock of faith Jesus always knew he could be, looks from disciple to disciple. "Believe in him. He's here. In this room. Right now."

John drinks deeply from the cup as Peter continues talking. "Remember what he told us: 'I am the way, the truth—'"

Jesus finishes the sentence: "'—and the life.'"

Peter spins around. Jesus stands in the doorway. The disciples are awestruck as he walks into the room.

Jesus has died on the cross as a sacrifice for the sins of all men. Throughout history, a lamb has been slaughtered for the same purpose. Jesus has been the Lamb of God, who takes away the sins of the world. He has conquered death.

Jesus says good-bye to his disciples after forty days back on earth. For three full years he has trained them, equipping them with the skills to lead others to follow in his footsteps and worship God. "You will receive power when the Holy Spirit comes to you," he tells them. "My body can be in only one place, but my Spirit can be with you all wherever you are. Go into the world and preach the Gospel unto all creation."

The disciples listen intently, knowing that this is the last time they will see Jesus. He is not saying that the Holy Spirit will come into them right now, so they know they must wait for this great moment. Jesus stands before them and gives them peace. Everything he said would happen has come to pass, and it is clear that the power of God extends much further than they even dared to believe. They have nothing to fear—even death. It is a proper and fitting way to say good-bye. Peter is anointed as the new leader of the disciples in Jesus' absence.

"Peace be with you," says Jesus.

The words echo in the disciples' ears. This peace pulses through them, infusing them with energy and calm resolve—this is the peace that will fortify them as they do God's work.

He then ascends into heaven.

Ten days later is the feast known as Pentecost.

This is a time of thanksgiving, when the Jewish people remember the bounty of the harvest.

For Caiaphas, this means a return to normal after the upheaval of Passover. From the temple steps, he watches with pleasure as daily life revolves around him:

pilgrims chatting in the streets, walking with sheaves of wheat, baskets of bread, and bundles of fruit and olives. These are the fruits of the harvest—fruits that will soon be lavished upon his temple.

"Anything I should know about?" Caiaphas asks his servant Malchus.

Roman soldiers can be seen on the fringes of the crowd, but there is no sign of the rebellion or rioting that marked Passover.

"The crowds are quiet," Malchus tells him. "The Romans are merely keeping watch."

"As it should be," he says, then pauses. "Any sign of Jesus' followers?"

"None."

"Really? Make sure the temple guards stand ready. If they return, you will have to deal with them."

But Jesus' disciples—now also known as the apostles—are gathering in Jerusalem, easily concealed among the hordes of pilgrims. Jesus has promised that the Holy Spirit will come to them, but they're not quite sure what that means. So they remain in their hiding place, waiting.

They look to Peter. "I know it's dangerous for us all to be here at once, but Jesus said that when two or three gather in his name, he would be with us." He sees that his words are having little effect. "Come, let us pray." Peter shuts his eyes. He reaches out and takes hold of the hands of the two disciples sitting on either side of him. "Our Father, who art in heaven, hallowed be thy name...."

John and the others pick up the words, and all join hands. "Your kingdom come, your will be done, on earth as it is in heaven."

The lamps in the room flicker and smoke as the prayer continues. The room grows suddenly dark. The wind outside rises, and the sound fills the room. Shutters bang open. Scared but unbowed, the disciples continue praying. Tongues of fire enter the room and settle upon each apostle. The Holy Spirit fills them. Soon all of them are praying in different languages, even though none of them have ever understood those tongues before. In this way, they are being prepared to go out unto all nations and preach the Word of God.

Empowered and renewed, the disciples march down the stairs and open the door. They scan the crowd for signs of Romans or Pharisees or temple guards. "People of Israel," says Peter, with a sense of poise and command that surprises all of the disciples. Peter has been radically changed by God's saving grace.

"God promised King David that one of his descendants would be placed upon his throne. A man whose flesh could not be corrupted. Now God has raised Jesus to life. Jesus of Nazareth is the Messiah. He is the Christ. Come join us!"

John chimes in, "Join us!"

The crowd roars in approval, chanting, "Jesus is the Lord." People clamor for Peter's blessing, reaching out to touch him. But the upheaval does not go unnoticed. Within moments, a Roman centurion hovers on the edge of the crowd.

"We're taking our chances here," John whispers to Peter.

"Jesus risked his life every day," responds Peter.

It is morning in Jerusalem, and yet another of the city's many beggars begins his day. The man's legs will not support him, so he uses his arms to drag himself to his usual spot. His knuckles are calloused and his skin filthy from years of the same ritual—dragging and then squatting, his body all too often coated in the grit and dust of a busy city going about its day.

A stranger drops a coin into his hand. The beggar nods in thanks but does not make eye contact.

Peter approaches. The beggar does not know him and holds out his hand, palm up. Peter stops and crouches down. The beggar looks at him with curious eyes, as if some great evil will befall him next. Peter has been trailed at a distance by a small crowd of new believers, and they edge closer, eager to see if Peter will do what they hope he will do. Peter and the beggar lock eyes. "I don't have silver or gold," Peter tells him. "But what I have, I will give to you." Peter raises his own palm to the sky. "In the name of Jesus Christ, our Lord and savior, I want you to stand." Peter places his right hand in that of the beggar. He lifts gently but then lets go. The beggar rises to his feet on his own power.

"It's a miracle," cries a voice in the crowd.

Peter responds by turning to face these new believers. "Why are you surprised? Do you think that he is healed by *my* power? Or by that of my fellow apostles? No. It is by Jesus' power that this man walks. Jesus is the Messiah!"

The beggar has a dizzy smile on his face, and walks around for the first time in his life.

"Jesus did this!" chants the crowd. "Jesus did this!"

Not far away, inside the great temple, the high priest Caiaphas hears the roar.

"What are they saying?" he asks Malchus. As always, his servant hovers just a few feet away. But Malchus doesn't get the chance to answer, for a furious Caiaphas has deciphered the sounds for himself. "Why are they chanting that wretched man's name?" Caiaphas demands. "Why!"

Malchus remains silent as Caiaphas launches into a furious rant. "We'll have the Romans down on us any minute. I told you to deal with these people before this could happen. And now it is done, and I am once again forced to deal with it. Bring the ringleaders to me!"

Within the hour, the temple guards have bound and beaten Peter and John. They drag the two into Caiaphas's chamber and hurl them to the floor. The healed beggar, now clearly terrified, is led in by the arm.

"Stand up," Caiaphas says crisply as he enters the room. He's just received word that more than five thousand people have become followers of Jesus since hearing the beggar was healed. This is an enormous figure. This must be stopped.

John and Peter struggle to their feet. They face Caiaphas, defiant.

"Tell me," demands the high priest, "what makes you think it acceptable to preach in the name of that dead criminal?"

"Jesus lives," Peter informs him.

"Impossible."

"This man walked because of the power of Jesus Christ," Peter reminds him.

"Really?" responds Caiaphas, trying to sound bemused. "Is this true?" he asks the beggar.

Malchus whispers to Caiaphas. "I have seen this man on the street for years. He has been lame his whole life, and…it is true."

Caiaphas pauses for an eternity, never moving his focus from Peter and John. Then he finally speaks: "I forbid you to talk of your so-called Messiah from this day forward."

"Judge for yourself whether it is better in God's sight to obey you rather than God," Peter responds.

"I have a duty to our temple, our nation, and our God!" Caiaphas responds angrily. "I repeat: you are forbidden from speaking about your Messiah!"

"We cannot help speaking about what we have seen and heard," says John.

"Then you will be beaten," Caiaphas threatens. "Either remain silent or suffer the same fate as your Jesus."

"We must obey God, rather than men," say the disciples, almost in unison.

No matter what code of silence he might try to enforce, Caiaphas senses he is powerless to stop this movement. People are turning their hearts to Jesus in record numbers. Caiaphas can't stop the five thousand, but he will silence the apostles, one by one—though not now. Reluctantly, Caiaphas lets Peter and John go.

The apostles meet secretly to regroup. Along with Mary Magdalene, they assemble in the small upper room that has marked their gatherings so many times. But this is not a time of peace or even connection. The disciples are engaged in a heated debate as to their future. A frightened Thomas dislikes the conflict, and he is on the verge of leaving just moments after his arrival. John, on the other hand, is in a particularly foul mood, eager to do battle.

"It's getting too dangerous," says Thomas. "If we stay in Jerusalem, we will die."

"I'm not afraid of death," John says defiantly.

"None of us are," says Peter, taking on the role of peacemaker. "But now is not the time. We cannot spread his Word if we are dead."

The disciples stop their bickering. Peter has their attention.

He takes a deep breath and begins to explain himself. "Jesus said, 'Preach to all creation.' Our job is now to spread the Word."

"I thought that's what we were already doing," challenges Thomas.

"And we have," Peter reminds him. "But now we must go out into the world, far beyond merely Jerusalem."

"Where will we go?" asks Mary.

"Where the spirit leads us," says Peter.

"I feel called to travel north—perhaps to Ephesus," says John. His eyes well with tears, as he knows death might await him once he steps out alone into the world.

The disciples arise. They take one another's hands and pray. This will be their last moment as a group. After so many years and so many world-changing experiences, their work now will be solitary and dangerous, without the comfort or support of this band of brothers.

John, with his gift for insight, offers perspective. "We will meet again," he tells them all. "On earth or in heaven."

One by one, the disciples say their good-byes, shedding many a tear and sharing more than one vivid memory. They have never considered themselves merely friends, but lifelong companions who have come together and given up everything in the name of Jesus. Their bond runs deep, which makes the good-byes all the more difficult.

They step out into the street and scatter. Their travels take them far and wide.

⌒

Thus the Gospel, as the words of Jesus are known, enters the Roman world. Peter is tireless in his work, as are all the other disciples. But one man does more than any to take the Word to the empire. It is a man who once tried hardest to crush Jesus' disciples: Paul. His past as a hunter of Christians is not easily forgotten. Many are doubtful of his claims that he has changed, and rightfully so, for their memories of loved ones spirited away in the night or trampled before their own children are all too vivid. But Paul repeats his story again and again: how Jesus appeared to him in a vision as he traveled on the road to Damascus. Now he knows that God's love flows through him and will transform hearts as his heart has been transformed. "I've changed," he says. "I once was blind, but now I see."

In one small church, a woman steps forth and spits into his face. "Liar!" she screams at him.

Paul does not wipe it off. "Please," he tells her and the others in the small room, "listen before you judge."

The room goes silent, but the suppressed rage has a

sound all its own that rings in everyone's ears and lies heavy upon their hearts.

Paul continues, afraid and yet also unafraid, knowing that he has no choice but to say what he is about to say. "I did what I did because I was certain that I was right. I was certain that I knew the will of God. As certain as you are now."

He looks around the room, knowing that he's bought a little time.

"But then Jesus came to me. Not in righteous anger or in judgments, but in love. His love."

Eyes moisten. Heads nod. Yes, they've felt this, too.

"Without love we are nothing," Paul tells them. "Love is patient. Love is kind. It is not jealous. It does not boast. It is not proud."

There are murmurs of discontent. What does this man know about love?

But Paul continues. "It keeps no record of wrongs. It rejoices with the truth, bears all burdens, believes all things, hopes all things, endures all things. When everything else disappears, there still remains faith, hope, and love. But the greatest of these, by far, is love."

One by one, members of the congregation rise from their seats and walk to Paul. It is difficult for them at first, touching this man whose fists have so often brought forth pain. But they soon reach out and hug him, accepting him and his teachings.

One man holds back. He is a learned man, clearly disturbed by Paul's words, and he wants to have an intellectual discussion of what they mean.

Finally, Paul addresses him. "You don't believe in God's love?" he asks.

"I do," says the man, whose name is Luke. "But I am a Greek. A Gentile. I know there are laws and rituals that I must follow first to become a Jew."

Paul's face grows stern. He shakes his head. "No. No. You don't need to become a Jew in order to know God's love. It is available to all."

"But the laws," Luke reminds him.

"If you could be saved just by following laws, Jesus would have died for nothing. But Jesus died to save you from sin. To save all of us from sin."

Once again, Paul addresses the entire congregation. "There is no longer Jew or Greek, male or female, slave or free person. We are all one in Jesus Christ."

These are world-changing words, and the congregation shouts back a heartfelt "amen" in agreement.

"Join us," Paul tells Luke. "God will be with you."

Paul is a radical and a revolutionary, preaching this new Gospel of Christianity with a fervor that puts his life in danger and sees him thrown into prison time after time. This new faith spreads across the Roman Empire, thanks to Paul's selfless and tireless zeal.

But once again, it is Peter whom God calls upon to do some of his hardest chores. Peter accepts the difficult task of traveling to the hub of the empire to change hearts and minds. Peter, the unlearned and uneducated fisher of men, is on his way to Rome. Like Daniel wandering into the lion's den. To a rational man, Peter's fate will most certainly be death. But as he walks slowly through the empire on his way to Rome, Peter reminds himself of the story of God and all of us. The words and stories give him strength and serve as a reminder of his purpose: "In the beginning, God embraced Abraham. From him came a family that became twelve tribes, which became a people and a nation. Now, through Jesus Christ, we must embrace the entire world."

Thus fortified, Peter enters Rome. The city is exotic and exciting, with the smells of spices from around the world wafting through the winding streets. He feels out of place and at first believes that his simple dress and foreign appearance mark him as an outsider. But then he realizes that as the hub of the empire, Rome is home to men from around the known world. All manner of dialect and mode of dress can be seen all around him. Peter may be an outsider, he realizes, but he is not alone.

～～～

Luke, the new follower whom Paul has recruited for Jesus, like Matthew and Mark before him, is fervent about writing down the story of Jesus so that it will be passed on through all generations. He is sitting alone in an upstairs room in Rome when he hears the thunder of an approaching army. Luke knows what this means, and instantly races into the room where Paul sits in prayer.

"Paul," Luke warns him. "They're coming for you."

Paul has been expecting this moment for years. Despite his many times in prison for his faith, something tells him that this will be his final journey. "Take them." He nods to Luke. "These words and letters need to survive." Luke grabs the scrolls and writings from the table.

Paul rises up, as defiant as he was when he once persecuted Christians. Roman footsteps can be heard charging up the stairs. "Go," he orders Luke. "Get out of here. You need to stay alive to continue our work."

Luke hesitates but then nods and climbs out through the balcony.

Paul is alone. For nearly three decades he has preached the Word of God. It has been a hard life, full of deprivation and suffering. Yet in all the chaos and carnage that has marked the growth of the Christian church, Paul knows that the Word will survive him. The Word is love. "I have fought the good fight," he reminds himself as he sits down to await his fate. "I have finished the race. I have kept the faith." He sighs. His time has come. He turns to face the soldiers as they rush into the room.

The parchment scrolls escape with Luke and form a large part of the New Testament.

John is the last disciple standing; the one who owns the gift of intuition is a living miracle. He has refused to accept the Roman emperor as his god and somehow survived all Roman attempts to kill him. He lives out his days in a small cave on an island off the coast of Asia Minor. It is a sparse home, but it is enough for this elderly disciple. The Romans could have killed him any of a number of ways, but they have exiled John to the remote island of Patmos. His face is weathered from the wind and the sun, and his lips are chapped from sunburn and thirst. The Romans assume that his isolation will mean death—that they will work him to death, as they have so many others. But John knows how to fish. He lives off the sea, confident that his life's work means descendants as numerous as the stars. The Romans may have sent him away, but like Christianity itself, they cannot wipe away his memories. Or his gift of intuition.

At his lowest ebb—and there are many in these final, lonely days—John has a revelation of hope. He looks back on the past, on all that has happened in the years since he met Jesus. He hears Jesus' voice as a memory, but the memory becomes clearer and clearer. His vision shifts from the past to the present, and then to the future—a future infinitely greater than anything that has come before. Jesus stands before him.

"I am the Alpha and the Omega," Jesus says, appearing to John in the small cave. A fish rests on the coals, waiting to be turned. "The first and the last, the beginning and the end."

John's face is transformed into joy. "Lord, forgive me. I have been expecting death, but it is you."

Jesus smiles. His hand beckons to John, leading him out of the cave. "There will be no more death or mourning or crying or pain," Jesus tells him. "I will make everything new." He offers John a cup of water, which the disciple slowly lifts to parched lips. "To him who is thirsty, I will give water from the river of life. Behold, I am coming soon. For I am the light of the world."

An ecstatic John understands fully what Jesus is telling him.

"Blessed are those who read the words of the book," Jesus tells him. "And heeds the words that are written in it. May the grace of the Lord be with all God's people."

"Amen," John whispers. He looks into Jesus' eyes, eyes that saw the beginning of time. They saw Adam and Eve; they saw Noah and Abraham and David. They also see the future: billions of Jesus' followers—as numerous as the stars in the sky—repeating the word that John has just whispered.

"Amen."